Also by M. Scott Kelley

Rose City Demise

Rose City Risk

M. Scott Kelley

AuthorHouse™
1663 Liberty Drive
Bloomington, IN 47403
www.authorhouse.com
Phone: 1-800-839-8640

First published by AuthorHouse 02/24/2011

ISBN: 978-1-4567-3873-0 (sc)
ISBN: 978-1-4567-3872-3 (hc)
ISBN: 978-1-4567-3871-6 (e-b)

Library of Congress Control Number: 2011903028

Printed in the United States of America

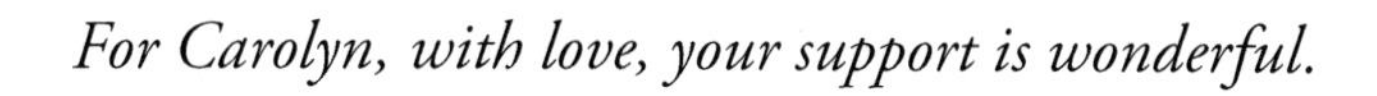

For Carolyn, with love, your support is wonderful.

I

My cast was perfect and the feeling of satisfaction I had was almost, but not quite, as good as when I actually hooked up. I was fishing for winter steelhead on the Clackamas River near Carver outside Portland, Oregon on a perfect Monday in early March. It would have been a perfect day even if I hadn't already landed and released two of the incredibly beautiful fish I was targeting. The fact the bite was on and the sky a deep blue made it one of those days that I live for. One of the most rewarding benefits of being a private investigator and being my own boss was that I could take time for days such as this. It far more than made up for the somewhat meager income I managed to derive from the times I actually did work. This is not to say that I find what I do for a living unrewarding, because it often is, especially when I helped decent people out of tough situations.

I had been fishing since daybreak and I could tell it was about time to call it a day. Traffic was picking up on the bridge near my fishing spot with people heading in for their jobs in the city and its environs. It was tough to call it quits because I had the prime drift to myself for a change. The steelhead is a large sea going member of the salmon family. The run was just about over and I wanted to make the most of it. I was in between jobs and had nothing significant pending, so I told myself, as so many anglers had through the ages, just one more cast and that will be it. Once again I zipped my custom made spinner out into the riffle and let it sink before starting a slow retrieve. Once again I felt the lure bounce along the bottom, come to a suspiciously fishy feeling stop, and I set the hook. With steelhead you have no doubt when you have a fish on and my line screeched off the ultra light reel as the fish took off with a vengeance.

It was at that moment that my cell phone started jingling with the customized ring I had selected for my significant other, Holly Palmer. Holly was probably the only person whose call I would answer given I had a fish on (and I almost included my mother in that). Few people or things are more important to me than fishing but Holly is one of them. I loosened my drag and tucked my fishing rod under my arm hoping for the best. Given I had told Holly what my plans were for the morning and that she knew how I felt about fishing I knew her call had to be important.

"Hey, Holly, what's up?" I asked with what I hoped sounded like sincere interest. She answered, sounding upset which was extremely unusual for her, by saying, "Matt, sorry to call but I have some terrible news. Alex's friend Doug was found dead near the Burnside Bridge. Alex just called and I told her I would give you a call and see if you could check with Ben and see what the police know." Alex, short for Alexandra Galloway, was Holly's best friend and they worked together as sports apparel designers at Nike.

Ben, otherwise known as Detective Canfield, was a homicide detective with the Portland Police. He and I had met while I was working on a case the previous fall and we had since become friends outside our working relationship. I told Holly I would call and check in with him and call her back. She thanked me and asked how the fishing was. I told her it had been fantastic and that I'd fill her in later if she was willing. She told me that would be great, I could hear her customary good cheer returning, and we hung up.

I put away my phone and began to retrieve my line which, as I expected, had gone slack. The fish was long gone. I knew the fishing spell was broken and it was time to get back to the real world.

II

I WADED BACK TO the beach and trudged up to my green Toyota Tundra pickup. Not for the first time I wondered how a great person such as Alex could fall for a ne'er-do-well like Doug Peterson. Doug was a spoiled only child of rich parents who, at least in my humble opinion, had been born with a silver spoon in his mouth and grown up with no regard for others. Holly and I had often tried to talk each other into speaking to Alex about breaking it off with Doug but we had always concluded this was one of those things we just couldn't do. We hoped Alex would come to her senses without being too badly hurt but it sounded as if that decision had been taken away from her.

Once I had taken off my chest waders and pulled on sneakers I pulled out my cell phone. I dialed up my best buddy who was on a vacation fly fishing for snook in Honduras and left him a quick message letting him know he wasn't the only one catching fish. After hanging up I punched in Detective Canfield's cell number and waited for him to answer. He picked up and said, "Hey Matt, I bet I know why you are calling. Doug Peterson, right?" I told him yes and asked how he knew. He said that he had just spoken to Alexandra and she had dropped my name. They had set up an appointment for 8:30 for Alex to meet with Ben at Central Precinct for the usual questioning given Alex and Doug's relationship. Alex had asked if I could sit in with her. Ben said, "I was just reaching for my phone to call you to see if you could make it but you beat me to the punch. How about it? Can you get down here?" I looked at my watch and saw it was 7:20 which left me time to get downtown if I hustled so I told I'd be there and we hung up.

I started up my truck and swung out of the parking lot and across the bridge and I found myself speculating on how Doug had come to grief. The Burnside Bridge area was a fairly notorious spot right smack in downtown Portland. I could easily envision it being a random act of violence, a mugging gone badly for example, but of course I had no information to base that on. I set such speculation aside as futile and fired up the iPod that was hooked up to my stereo and cranked up a classic rock playlist I had put together. The transition from idyllic early morning fishing to Tom Petty's *Runnin' Down a Dream* was fairly abrupt but I hadn't had enough coffee and didn't have time to stop.

III

TRAFFIC WAS NOT BAD and I parked near Central Precinct with ample time to stop in a Starbucks across the street from the precinct and pick up some caffeinated drinks. I figured we'd all need them. I knew from experience what Ben drank, triple mocha, and called Holly to bring her up to speed and get some input on Alex's coffee drink of choice. Holly told me Alex was partial to vanilla lattes so I added that to my order.

I managed to work my way through the downtown sidewalk rush without spilling anything and walked into the small foyer just in time to see Alex walking towards the window that separated the public area from reception desk. I called to her and she turned and gave me a glad smile and said, "Matt, thank you so much for coming. I feel so much better knowing I have a friend here." I reached out my free hand and took one of hers, gave it a squeeze and said simply, "Sorry about Doug. I'm glad to help in any way I can." She returned the squeeze and blinked away some tears and swallowed as if to clear her throat but did not speak. I noticed that despite having obviously had a tough time she still looked very good. She was a natural Irish beauty with wavy red hair and piercing green eyes.

I handed her the latte and said, "I called Holly and she told me this is your coffee drink of choice. I think you might need this because these sessions can be fairly trying. That said I know Ben well enough to tell you that he is fair and a true professional. You don't have to worry about him pulling any bad cop type routine, if that is any consolation."

She took a grateful sip and nodded, "Thanks for this and thanks for the reassurance. I admit to feeling apprehensive just being here." With that we both turned to the receptionist and I told him that we had an appointment to see Detective Canfield. He nodded, picked up the phone, dialed a number and spoke briefly. As he hung up he said, "Sure, the detective said he'd be right down to take you both up." We thanked him and walked away to talk out of earshot.

I said, "Alex, how much do you know about what happened? If you'd rather wait until Ben shows up so you don't have to repeat yourself I'd understand." She shook her head and said, "No, I don't mind talking mostly because I really don't have much to say. Doug and I went out to dinner and he dropped me off at my place around nine thirty. He said he had some business to take care of. That's the last time I saw or spoke to him. His father Earl called me very early this morning to give me the news that Doug had been found dead. He did not have any details himself and we hung up after a very short conversation. Doug and his father were not close. I had the sense that Earl was feeling more rage than anguish about Doug's death. I hope you don't mind that I mentioned your name and business to him. I don't know if he'll follow up, but I wanted to give you a heads up."

At that moment Ben stepped through one of the glass doors that led to the restricted area and motioned us over. I shook hands with Ben and turned to Alex and said, "Alex, this is Detective Canfield. Detective, this is Ms. Galloway." I kept it deliberately formal until I could get a sense of how both of them wanted to proceed. Ben quickly solved that as he shook Alex's hand and said, "Ms. Galloway, thank you for coming in so promptly. I hope this is not too difficult for you?"

Alex shook her head no and responded, "No, I just hope that whatever I can tell you will be helpful. I was just telling Matt that I'm not sure that I know anything that will be of any use."

"Well, you'd be surprised how often people say that at the beginning of an investigation like this and it turns out they are able to provide valuable information." With that Ben turned and led us to an elevator. He hit the up button and the doors slid right open. He motioned for us to proceed and we did so. The three of us rode up to the sixth floor in silence. When the doors had opened, Ben said politely, "Please follow me." He led us to a small room with a table and four chairs. He shut the door behind us and asked us to be seated. He waited until Alex sat down before seating himself. I set his mocha down in front of him and he looked up with a smile and a nod and then I took a seat myself next to Alex.

"Ms. Galloway, I'd first like to make sure you know you are not here because you are under suspicion. This is simply an informational back and forth. That said, if you do feel you would like legal counsel present, you are free to stop at any time and place a call. Is that okay with you?"

Alex looked at me and I gave her an encouraging grin and she turned to Ben and said, "Yes, that is clear and I am fine with proceeding. I am not at all certain how this will go. I've never had any dealings with the police. That is why I asked Matt to sit in."

"Okay, how long did you know Mr. Peterson? I'd also like to hear about the last time you saw him," Ben asked, taking a notepad and pen out of his shirt pocket.

Alex replied, "I've known Doug for about eight months. We met at a charity event for the Washington Park Zoo. I was just telling Matt that Doug and I had dinner last night. We went to Jake's and finished there at about 9pm. Doug said he had some business to take care of so he dropped me off at my condo at about 9:30 or so."

Ben nodded as he jotted some brief notes and asked, "Did Mr. Peterson give you any idea of the nature of his business that night? Did he mention any names or say where he was going?"

Alex shook her head no and said, "Doug was never very open about his business dealings, Detective. I know he was in some financial difficulty which was very hard for him. You may know that his parents are quite well to do. Doug did not want to follow in his father's footsteps and repeatedly said he wanted to make his own way. He often expressed his frustration with his situation."

Ben asked, "Do you know what sort of business Mr. Peterson was in? Did he work regular hours? Anything along these lines that you can tell me would be helpful."

Alex responded, "Well, I hate to admit it but Doug did not seem to work on any regular schedule. He was always talking about some big deals he had in the works and that he was close to making a big score that would set him up. It seems odd that I know as little as I do given our relationship. This was not something we spoke much about. Doug kept his cards close to his chest. I do know that Doug spent a fair amount of time at Portland Meadows and he took horse racing very seriously."

If I hadn't known Ben as well as I did, I would have missed his increase in interest at this information. I was aware that Doug had been a bit of a gambler at the horse track. The few times he, Alex, Holly, and I had gotten together socially he often went on and on about racing and how close he'd been on such and such a race. I found this quite tedious as I had little interest in horse racing myself. This was one of several reasons the four of us did not get together very often.

"Did you ever go to the track with him, Ms. Galloway?" asked Ben. Alex nodded and said, "Yes, but not very often. I do enjoy watching the horses, such beautiful animals, but the gambling part of it did not do much for me."

Ben asked, "Did Mr. Peterson associate with anyone in particular the times you did go to the track with him?" Alex nodded and said, "There was one man we saw on a few occasions. Doug introduced us on a first name basis. I think the guy's name was Jonathan, but I did not hang around the two of them when they got together. I was somewhat uncomfortable around Jonathan. He was one of those guys who exuded the feeling he was god's gift to women and that I should acknowledge that. I'm not sure I'm explaining that very well, but I usually excused myself on some pretense or another when we met."

"I think I understand," said Ben, "Let's shift gears here a bit. Did you ever meet Mr. Peterson's family? If you did can you give me any insight into their relationship?" He sat back and took a deep drink of his mocha.

"Yes, I met Doug's parents and the four of us socialized several times. We usually met for dinner at their house, but would occasionally meet for dinners out. His father's name is Earl. He is some sort of financial advisor with a firm called Unlimited Horizons Investing. His mother's name is Eleanor. She doesn't work, but is very involved in various charities and clubs. She was one of the main organizers of the event for the Washington Park Zoo where I first met Doug. Doug was an only child and I never met or heard about any other relatives. I think his parents tried to have other children but there were complications that I did not fully understand and certainly wasn't going to ask about. I know that Doug and his father were not close. There was a great deal of tension between them when they were together. Doug and his mother seemed to get on well together though. I'm sure that if not for that Doug would have had very little use for seeing his family. Doug often spoke with bitterness that his father treated him with condescension and that he had limited patience. I'm afraid it was one of those all too common father-son relationships where the son felt he never lived up to expectations." Alex paused to take a drink of her latte and continued, "The times the four of us spent together were usually uncomfortable. Most of the conversation was between Doug and his mother. I tried to ease the tension but was rarely successful."

Ben nodded contemplatively and flipped to a new page in his notebook. I knew he took copious notes and could recreate fairly complex conversations he'd heard while working. I also knew he had a very keen mind and missed very little of what he heard or observed. After a pause he continued, "Ms. Galloway, can you tell me about any other people Mr. Peterson interacted with socially? I know this may sound clichéd, but did he have any enemies?"

Alex took another sip of her coffee and then said, "Doug was kind of a loner. I did not know any of his friends and he rarely spoke of anyone he socialized with when we were not together. I'm certainly not aware that he had any enemies. Doug and I did socialize occasionally with Matt and his friend, dinners out and to clubs to listen to music, but not frequently. As I sit here and listen to myself I'm amazed just how little I knew of Doug. When he and I were together we mostly talked about my work and family. He was a very private person and had a side that I don't think very many people got to see."

Ben turned to me and asked, "Matt, given you knew Mr. Peterson, I'm wondering if you can think of anything you'd like to add? Did the two of you ever meet outside the foursome?"

I shook my head negatively and firmly stated, "No, Doug and I never met socially other than with Alex and Holly. We did not really have anything in common other than both knowing Alex. I really can't think of anything I can add to help you."

Ben looked at me and I shrugged and said, "Sorry, Ben, but Doug and I were just too different to do other than exchange pleasantries." He flipped back to the first page of his notes and quickly scanned them and said, "Well Ms. Galloway, I think I've taken enough of your time for now. I could easily come up with some follow up questions as I continue the investigation though. May I call you as I need to?"

Alex looked a bit surprised but said, "Of course. Feel free to call me at any time. Here is my business card and I'll jot my cell phone number on the back." She did so and slid the card across the table.

Ben stood up and put the card in his shirt pocket and said, "Thank you for your cooperation Ms. Galloway. I'll walk you to the elevator if I may? Do you mind sticking around for a moment or so, Matt?" I told him that would be fine and said to Alex, "Are you headed to work?" She nodded, and I asked her if she wanted to get together for lunch with Holly and me. She nodded again, gratefully this time I thought, and said, "Yes, that would be great. I could use the company to be honest." I said, "Fine, I'll give Holly a call and set up the details with her."

With that Ben opened the door for Alex and they both walked out. Ben returned in a few moments and closed the door behind him. He sat down and finished off his mocha in a couple of swallows and set his empty cup down. "Okay, Matt, I wasn't sure if you were holding out on your answer and wanted to see if you had anything to add now that Ms. Galloway is gone?"

I chuckled at him and said, "Boy, being observant is a pretty good trait for a police officer. The truth is I thought Peterson was a pretty shallow person who was very self-absorbed. I thought Alex deserved much better and while I wouldn't wish his end on anyone, I think Alex will be much better off without him. She is a terrific person and a good friend of Holly's and mine."

Ben leaned back in his chair and said, "Well, I'm obviously comfortable accepting your opinion of her, but have to ask if you think her capable of being complicit in murder?" I shook my head vehemently and said, "Impossible. I'd stake my bottom dollar that Alex is completely off that hook. She is a very caring and open person and if she knew anything about Peterson's death we could tell right away. I'd advise you to cross her off your list of suspects right now and look elsewhere."

Ben nodded started to say something but checked himself and said, "Sure, your comments match my first impressions, but you know the drill. I also have to ask if you are officially involved in this case?" I shook my head and answered, "Nope, but I haven't really had any time to speak to Alex other than a few moments before we first saw you this morning. I'm sure she will be content to let you and your compatriots do your jobs. Next time I see you will probably be for racquetball this weekend." We both stood up and walked out the door and he hit the elevator button for me. We waved at each other as the doors slid closed. Little did I know that I was as wrong as I could be. I would become very much involved in his investigation before all was said and done.

IV

I PULLED MY CELL phone out of my pocket when I got to the sidewalk in front of the police station and dialed Holly. She picked up and said, "Alex just called and said you were all done with Ben and that she's headed in to the office. How'd it go from your perspective?"

I answered her by saying, "Well, Ben didn't get as detailed as I thought he might, but I think he got a couple of tidbits from Alex that he will follow up on. I'm sure he's just pulling together as many threads as he can right now and will follow all of them up very carefully if he feels he needs to. I asked Alex if she wanted to have lunch with us figuring she'd want company. Are you up for that?"

She answered in what I knew was a mock serious tone, "Let's see, lunch with two of my favorite people. I guess I can make it. Just tell me when and where and Alex and I will meet you there."

I thought for a moment and said, "It's been a while since we've had Thai, how about Golden Pagoda at noon? I'll get there a tad early and get us a table." She quickly agreed and said, "Alex and I have eaten there several times. I know she likes the coconut curry chicken. If you want to just order two of those for us that'd be okay." With that we said goodbye and I hung up wondering if I was up for the challenge of the Pagoda's volcano squid. I answered my own question with a resounding "yes", knowing a couple of cold Singha beers would quench the internal flames.

That important issue settled I looked at my watch and saw it was only ten o'clock. I had plenty of time for a swim and a shower before meeting the lovely ladies and wanted to make sure I got whatever lingering fishy odors off of me so as not to spoil any appetites. I got in my truck, keyed the ignition, and pulled away from the curb. My club was near down town and not ten minutes from the precinct.

I carded in, smiled hello to the very cute front desk clerk who smiled back looking young enough to make me feel my own thirty-two years keenly, and headed to the locker room. I quickly changed, rinsed off in the shower and headed to the pool. Swimming was not only a great solo work out but it came naturally enough to me that I could clear my mind and focus not on swimming itself, but whatever issue I wanted to. I made a nice clean entry dive and as I made my first flip turn I wondered what Ben had been about to say just before we parted. It helped to be observant if your profession was being a private investigator too.

V

I SWAM HARD FOR a solid hour and jumped out of the pool feeling invigorated. Knowing I was going to be seeing Holly soon was also invigorating and I smiled to myself. It dawned on me that she was probably thinking similar thoughts about seeing me which made my smile broaden. Fearing if I kept that up I'd break out into outright laughter and have the few other people in the pool area looking at me strangely, I set those thoughts aside and went about the business of showering, drying off, and getting changed. I kept a permanent locker at the club and always kept a change of clothes there just for occasions such as this.

The same young woman was at the front desk and she looked up as I approached and said brightly, "Have a great rest of the day, Mr. MacKinnon!" I stopped, stuck out my hand and said, "You can call me Matt. You are new here aren't you?" She shook my hand with a nice firm grip and responded, "Yes, this is my first day and so far so good. My name is Monique. Do you come here often?"

"Yep, I make it in about five or six times a week for swimming or racquetball. Nice to meet you, Monique, and I'll see you next time." I walked away whistling U2's *It's a Beautiful Day* hoping she was old enough to know the tune.

The Golden Pagoda was far enough away that I chose to drive so I jumped in my truck and headed off. I did arrive just early enough to beat most of the noontime rush and grabbed a table just ahead of a group of what looked like Portland State University coeds. The waiter, who had worked there for years and was well acquainted with my usual orders, didn't wait, but brought over a Singha and asked, "Just you today, Matt? Are you expecting someone else?" I responded, "Holly and our friend Alex will be here in a few, Chan. Holly asked me to order a couple of coconut curry chickens and I'll have the volcano squid. If you see me with an empty bottle just bring another as fast as possible because you know what the squid does to me." Chan laughed and said, "You bet, Matt. Coming right up. I'll keep an eye on you."

The door opened and I was aware of the special feeling I always felt when I saw Holly. I waved at her and was rewarded with a glorious smile I felt in my toes. I stood as she and Alex walked up and I gratefully accepted a peck on the cheek from her. I helped them both into their chairs, with more panache than usual, sat down across from them, and said, "Order is placed and should be right up. It is nice to see you in better circumstances, Alex. Meeting at the police station is something we should avoid from here on okay?"

Alex grinned and said, "That's a deal Matt. Thank you again for taking time to be there for me. Having you there took the edge off the interview but I do have to say I was impressed with Detective Canfield. He struck me as a pretty solid character and a very nice guy."

I turned to Holly and said, "How's the morning?" She answered, "It was fine but certainly not as eventful as yours. I gathered from your tone on the phone when I first called that you had some luck. How many fish did you catch?" I filled them both in with more detail than they were probably looking for even though both women enjoyed fishing themselves. As I finished Chan walked up and set our food and another beer down in front of us. He asked the two women if they wanted anything besides water to drink. They both ordered Singha beer.

The three of us set to with gusto and the conversation lagged. The relative silence was filled only with sporadic comments from all of us along the lines of, "please pass the hot sauce, how about a napkin, and wow this is spicy". Pausing for a moment to mop my sweaty forehead I said, "Alex, do you mind talking about what happened this morning? You know my business and can probably understand why I'm interested."

She shook her head, took a respectable swig of her beer, and said, "No, it actually makes me feel better to talk about it. I also have something I want to tell the two of you." Holly and I looked at her expectantly and she continued, "I know how the two of you felt about Doug. I could tell you were struggling with not speaking to me about your thoughts and I want you to know I appreciate that you didn't unload on me. I like to think that knowing when not to speak up when a person is messing up is a sign of a solid friendship. Truth be told, I was getting my nerve up to tell Doug I wanted to break it off. That was one reason I was so upset with what happened. I felt completely guilty for not being up front with him. As I said at the police station Doug, did have a side to him that he let few people see, but it was hard to find and much too small a part of him. I want a relationship like the two of you have, more caring and joy filled." Holly reached across the table and gave Alex's hand a quick squeeze and she tapped my shin with her foot under the table. Alex paused to dab at her eyes, tear filled not from the spicy food but emotion, and continued, "There, I've said what I wanted to say and sorry to be a downer. What do you want to know, Matt?"

I forked my last bit of rice and pushed my plate away and said, "Alex, would it make you feel better if I poked around to see if I can dig up anything I can turn over to Ben? I'd be happy to do so if you like."

At that moment Alex's cell phone started to jingle and she said, "I'd better see if this is Detective Canfield calling, okay?" I nodded and she pulled her phone out, looked at it and said, "Oh, this is actually Doug's mother. I'd better see what's up." She popped the phone open and spoke into it. "Hello, Eleanor, how are you?" She stopped to listen for a few moments and then said, "Yes, I did go in and speak to the police and it went okay. I couldn't tell them much though." She paused again and her eyebrows arched and she said, "Why it happens that he is sitting right across the table from me. We are just finishing lunch. Yes, I will ask him." She punched the mute button and stated, "Matt, talk about timing. Doug's mother is interested in talking to you about looking into Doug's death. She would like to speak to you, okay?"

I nodded and held out my hand. Alex passed across the phone. Trying to sound professional, I said, "This is Matt MacKinnon, Mrs. Peterson. I'm sorry for your loss." A smooth, very self assured voice responded by saying, "Thank you, Mr. MacKinnon. I happened to be listening in when my husband spoke to Alex this morning. I heard her give my husband your name and phoned Alex to see if she had your number. A detective was just here at my home and he asked many questions about my son. He seemed a competent sort of police officer but I know the police are extremely busy. I want to do anything I can to bring my son's murderer to justice." Her voice caught at that moment and I could envision her collecting herself. I did not speak but gave her time to continue which she did after a momentary pause. "Are you able to come and visit with me sometime this afternoon?"

I said, "Sure, we are just finishing lunch. I need to clear some things with Alex and I can get directions to your home from her. May I assume you'll be home this afternoon, or would you like me to call to confirm I will come over?" She said she had no intentions of going anywhere and hung up with a cultured goodbye. I closed Alex's phone and handed it back across the table to her. "Well, Alex, I think you got the gist of that conversation. Of course having just offered to look into this case for you, I want to make sure you are okay with me potentially going to work for Mrs. Peterson. I'm perfectly willing to tell her I'm not available to go to work for her if you'd rather."

Alex said, "That is kind of you to offer, Matt, but I have no problem with you going and talking to Eleanor. She has far more at stake in this than I do. Thanks for asking though."

I nodded and asked for directions to the Peterson home, which she provided on a piece of paper she pulled from her purse. I asked for a few clarifications and then we all stood up to go. I stopped at the counter and paid the bill and gave a thumb up to Chan's brother who I could see through the window to the food preparation area. He waved a wire whisk at me and shouted, "Come back soon, Matt!"

Holly, Alex, and I paused on the sidewalk outside the Golden Pagoda and Holly said, "Thanks for lunch Matt. Will I see you after work?" I told her absolutely and also told Alex I'd keep her up to speed as things developed and she thanked me as well. We parted with smiles all around and I drove off towards the Peterson home lost in thought. I knew I could be in for a tough afternoon session with Mrs. Peterson given the emotional trauma she'd suffered.

VI

The Peterson home was an impressive structure in the Heights above Portland. The curving driveway was bounded by well landscaped grounds and the lot was set with several very large Douglas fir trees. The front of the home was mostly glass which I could understand given the view of the city and Willamette River below. I parked and walked up to the door and pushed the doorbell. After a short wait the door was opened by an attractive middle aged woman in khaki slacks and white blouse. I noticed that her eyes were somewhat red and slightly puffy but did not think anything of it. She said, "Good afternoon. I assume you are Mr. MacKinnon?"

I answered, "Yes, I am. Are you Mrs. Peterson?" She shook her head no and said, "No, my name is Gillian Anderson and I am Ms. Peterson's personal assistant. Ms. Peterson is in her office. Please follow me." With that she turned and walked down a hallway paneled in what I thought was white oak. She stopped at a door, knocked, and a muffled voice said, "Come in." She opened the door, entered, and said, "Ms. Peterson, this is Mr. MacKinnon."

A woman stood up and walked from behind a desk where she had been sitting. I guessed her to be in her late 50s but she carried herself very well and appeared to be in good shape. She was wearing a peach colored silk blouse and a matching skirt that came to her knees. The outfit was topped off with a simple string of pearls that probably cost more than my house. As she approached she held out her hand in a way that made me think she wanted me to kneel and kiss her knuckles. I decided against that but simply took her hand and gave a firm shake.

She said, "Thank you for coming over so promptly, Mr. MacKinnon. My name is Eleanor Peterson. Please sit down." She gestured to a couple of comfortable looking chairs set near a coffee table. "Can Gillian bring you anything? Coffee perhaps?"

I said, "Sure, a cup of coffee would be great if it is convenient. Black would be fine." Ms. Anderson said she would be right back and left. She was good to her word and she returned very quickly with a tray which held a coffee service and a small plate of sugar cookies. She poured what smelled like heavenly coffee for both of us and dropped two sugar cubes into Ms. Peterson's cup without being asked. "Will there be anything else Ms. Peterson?" She was answered with a polite "no, thank you" from her employer, who then said she'd ring if she wanted anything else. With that the personal assistant smiled and left, closing the door behind her.

We both raised our cups and I found the brew to be as good as expected. Ms. Peterson set her cup down and said, "Mr. MacKinnon, you can imagine how difficult this morning was. I'm still in shock from the news of my son's death. I understand you were present when Ms. Galloway was interviewed by the police. Did you think the police learned anything of value?"

I cleared my throat and had the fleeting thought that my thinking I'd be in for an emotional discussion with a bereft mother could not have been more off base. I said, "Ms. Peterson, I expect that the police are working very diligently to bring your son's killer to justice. I'm not sure what they gleaned from the discussion with Ms. Galloway and I'm not sure I'm the best person to ask. It might be advisable if you directed such questions to Detective Canfield, who is in charge of the investigation."

"Yes, I can understand that you would defer me to the police. I understand from Ms. Galloway's comment this morning while she was speaking to my husband that you are a private investigator. Is that correct?" I took another sip of coffee and answered, "Yes, that's correct."

She said with apparent interest, "I've never had a reason to hire a private investigator. What sort of credentials do you have? I assume there is a license required?"

I nodded and said, "Yes, I am licensed with the State and have worked with the police on a few capital cases. I've also done quite a bit of work that did not involve the police. If it helps I can assure you that my discretion is guaranteed. I can also say that I am by no means the only private investigator in the city. If you like I can give you a couple of other names of people I have worked with and whom I have found very competent." I was in no rush to appear eager, and found myself almost wishing she would take me up on my offer.

Instead she shook her head, "No, I did not mean to imply that I was questioning your bona fides, Mr. MacKinnon. I have a high regard for Ms. Galloway and if you are a friend of hers that's good enough for me. Perhaps I should just get to the point. I would like to engage your services, if you are available. As I said on the phone I am sure the police will do their best, but I want to assure myself that everything that can be done to catch my son's murderer is being done." At this the first crack in her façade appeared and her eyes closed briefly. After a short pause in which she clenched her fists she continued, "I want to be sure that someone is dedicating 100% of their time in pursuing this matter. Can you do this for me?"

I nodded and said, "Yes, I can. I have to tell you that I will ask a lot of questions. I can't be bound in any way from pursuing whatever thread I think might lead to answers. Of course I will report what I learn to you but I will also have to turn anything pertinent I discover to the police. If those basic ground rules work for you then I'm on board." I finished off my coffee and looked at her expectantly.

She nodded contemplatively and said, "Yes, I do like to understand just what the rules are and appreciate your directness. I do agree to your conditions. I just want as prompt a resolution to this issue as possible." With that we settled on the financial details and she signed a check for the balance. I thanked her and we stood. She opened the door for me and I said, "My first steps will be to talk to the police and get some details on what happened. I will definitely let them know that I'm working for you and that they know I'll cooperate with them fully. I've a pretty good relationship with the detective in charge and want to ensure that continues. After that I'll be asking a lot of questions and will probably call on you again as well." She nodded and saw me to the front door. We shook hands and I stepped outside. She closed the door firmly behind me.

VII

As I drove away from the Peterson house I looked at my watch and saw it was only two o'clock. I had plenty of time to check in with Ben Canfield before meeting Holly for dinner. I pulled off to the side of the road, parked and took my phone out of my pocket. I punched in Ben Canfield's cell number. He picked up after a couple of rings. "Hey, Matt, why am I not surprised to hear from you? Let me guess, you volunteered to work on this thing for Ms. Galloway, right?"

I could tell he was grinning as he said that, so I was happy to take him down a peg and said in an aloof tone, "I'll have you know I'm gainfully employed by Ms. Peterson, the victim's mother. I've just left her home and am wondering if you have time to chat about the case. She was actually fairly impressed with you, assuming it was you who spoke to her this morning, but wants to make sure all her bases are covered." I debated admitting that I had in fact offered to volunteer to work for Alex but decided not to give him the satisfaction.

"Yeah, Dave and I actually did the interviews with the parents together." The Dave he referred to was Detective Dave Richmond who often partnered up with Ben and who I'd worked with in the past. "I have to say they are a couple of cool customers. If I didn't know better I'd think we were investigating a routine theft and not the murder of their son." I could sense he was shaking his head in disbelief as he continued, "We met the father at his office downtown and then met with the mother at their home. How far have you gotten?"

"I just finished getting hired by Ms. Peterson, so am coming up to speed. I know you have got to be busy, but can I pick your brain on what facts you have so far?" He agreed and we set a meeting at a coffee bistro we frequented. I started up my truck, hit play on my iPod, and pulled back into traffic to the pounding rhythm of Kenny Wayne Shepherd's blues guitar.

I got to the bistro before Ben and stopped at the counter and bought a couple of grande house blends and oatmeal raison cookies, still feeling virtuous after my pre-lunch swim. Ben came through the door just as I sat down and I waved him over. He was about my size, five foot eleven and 200 pounds, but whereas I have brown hair and hazel eyes, Ben had black hair and dark brown eyes. He sat down and asked, "I assume one of these is for me?" I nodded and he voiced his thanks and then got down to business.

"Okay, here's what we know. One of our foot beat uniforms on routine early morning patrol called in the body at 6 am. He sealed off the area and Dave and I got there within half an hour. It was pretty bad Matt. The M.E. confirmed Peterson had been beaten up before being shot to death. We were able to recover a bullet. It looks like a smaller caliber, maybe a .32. Time of death around 2 am give or take an hour or so. Not surprisingly, given where the body was found, the guy's wallet was missing. We identified the body from a label sewed into his sport coat. As you might have guessed, there were a few street people in the area and we have questioned most of the ones who were hanging around. As you could also guess, none of them know anything and they'd barely even talk to us. We haven't given up on that angle and have some uniforms still working on that. The last person we know to have seen the guy alive was your friend Ms. Galloway who, as you heard, was dropped off at about 9:30. That obviously leaves a pretty big gap in time from then until the estimated time of death. It doesn't seem likely that he'd have been walking around down in that neck of the woods so it could be the killing did not happen there. Of course you know we've interviewed the parents and we're working on developing a list of known acquaintances. The usual drill and we're nowhere so far. One comment that Ms. Galloway made that caught my interest is that Peterson spent time at Meadows. We've gotten some rumblings through the grapevine that things have taken a bit of a twist there. What I mean by that is that the gambling there has maybe gotten a bit more organized and serious. Some of our guys are looking into that but we've nothing firm as of now. Now, tell me if you know anything I should know?"

I shook my head and answered, "Probably nothing significant but Holly and I did have lunch with Alex Galloway. She told us that she had been working up to breaking it off with Peterson, but hadn't done so yet. My meet with the mother did not shed any light either. We really did not talk too much about her son and his habits because I wanted to start with you and make sure we weren't covering the same ground. My only inclination at this point is to try and find out where Peterson got his money. Based on Alex's comments, it sounded as if he was hurting for cash but had some deals in the works. Could be he was into some bad stuff? Did he have any prior convictions?"

Ben nodded and said, "Sure, that's what we're thinking as well, but it couldn't hurt if we worked on that at the same time. We did run his name and he came up clean. You might get people to open up when they wouldn't with us. Sometimes I think the average member of the public watches too many crooked cop shows on TV and they assume we're all bent."

I chuckled and said, "Well, Ben, if it is any consolation, I've spoken to two people today who you made a good impression on. Both Alex Galloway and Ms. Peterson had good things to say about you. Keep up the good work."

I was very surprised to see him blush, something that I'd never seen before, and the reason became clear when he admitted, "I found Alex Galloway to be the most beautiful woman I've ever seen. Having her good opinion is a good thing in my book. I'll have to be careful to keep my personal thoughts out of this. I have never been in a situation like this before." He shot me a stern look and said, "Of course I know you private detectives pride yourselves on your discretion. Let's be sure you stick to that shall we, good buddy?" He stated that in a joking tone but I could tell he was quite serious.

I held out my hands and said, "Hey, you've nothing to fear from me. Mum is the word. But I can't help but say I think the two of you would be a perfect match!" Now I knew what he hadn't said during our chat in the precinct earlier that morning. I clapped him on the shoulder and said earnestly, "Best of luck to you in that, Ben."

We finished off our drinks and cookies and headed out the door to the sidewalk. We parted with a handshake and promises to keep in close touch. Ben headed off to his unmarked police sedan and I got in my truck and set off up the road towards my house in the hills above downtown Portland. I figured I had plenty of time to figure out what to do for my dinner with Holly.

VIII

BY THE TIME I pulled into my driveway and parked, I knew what I was going to do for dinner. I'd decided on venison stroganoff, one of Holly's and my favorites, with fresh steamed broccoli and French bread. I had all the ingredients on hand, the venison from a Columbia Black Tail I'd taken with my bow on a friend's property near Nehalem, Oregon. I set to work so the sauce had time to simmer and get a good blend. I cranked up my stereo and was enjoying the Lynyrd Skynyrd classic *Sweet Home Alabama* when the phone rang. I turned down the music and answered with an upbeat hello. It was Holly and she said, "I'm just leaving the office. What did you have in mind for dinner?" I told her and she asked if she could bring anything. I told her no; just herself and her smile. She laughed and said that she'd be there in 30 minutes or so.

Having gotten off to a good start on the stroganoff I, decided I was due a reward so I hit the fridge and pulled out a Fosters lager. It might not go perfectly with stroganoff but it sure went along well with the music. Life is full of compromises. I trimmed the broccoli and cut it into pieces and put it in a steamer pan so it was ready to turn on. The bread was next and I cut it long ways and buttered, sprinkled fresh minced garlic and parmesan cheese on both halves and put the halves back together. I then wrapped the whole in tin foil and tossed it in the oven. Final prep was to get a pot of salted water set out for the egg noodles. I felt the urge for an appetizer and decided to whip up some smoked steelhead dip. In my mind there are few fish that smoke up as well as steelhead and I had practiced enough with fish I'd caught over the years that I had the smoking process down pat. I flaked the fish with a fork and then warmed up some cream cheese in the microwave for 30 seconds or so and mixed the two with some leftover minced garlic, sour cream, and Tabasco sauce. I sampled the mixture on a bagel crisp and decided it was perfect.

Just then I heard a couple of raps on the front door and Holly's voice calling out a happy, "Just me, did you wait for me?" I said, "Nope, I'm already digging in so you better get up here." She came around the corner into the kitchen and into my arms for a solid hug and offered her face up for a kiss which I gleefully bestowed on her. She made a face and said, "Ugh, beer and garlic, no more smooching unless I get some myself." I quickly accommodated her request and we set to the dip and beer with avid greed.

After a few moments Holly asked, "How did your meet with Ms. Peterson go? Are you working on the case?" I nodded and filled her in on the details of my conversation with my new client and with most, but not all, of the details of my conversation with Ben Canfield. She made a face and said, "Oh, Matt. This is such a terrible situation. I feel so badly for the Peterson's. Even if they don't show any emotion they've got to be hurting. What is your next move?"

I took a swig of Fosters and told her, "I hope to speak to the father and get a sense of him and Doug's relationship. Based on what Alex said, it was probably pretty bad but if I can get a better handle on it myself I may get some insight into what Doug was into before he was killed. I do want to find out where Doug's money came from. He obviously had some sort of income because the few times the four of us went out he always paid his share. The horse track angle is probably worth following up on. I'm not at all familiar with the ins and outs of horse betting but I can imagine there's a seedy side to it." I got up and turned on the broccoli and noodle water, gave the sauce a stir, and sat back down next to Holly on the couch. "Dinner in about 15, so don't spoil it by eating too much dip."

She gave me an arch look and said, "Well, if you're cutting off the snacks then what are we going to do while we wait for the pot to boil?" I caught her drift immediately and we leaned towards each other and exchanged some very tangy kisses. Holly backed away and took a deep breath and said, "That is better, now we both taste like garlic. Let's finish up this dinner so we can take up where we just left off."

The two of us had worked together in the kitchen often enough that we were an efficient team. She set the table while I took care of the final steps in dinner prep. As we worked, we exchanged details of how our days had gone which for me included bringing her fully up to speed on my meeting Gillian Anderson and Mrs. Peterson. It wasn't long before we dished up and sat at the small table in my dining room. Dinner was as good as I hoped and Holly rewarded me with sighs of contentment. When we were finished we quickly cleaned up and put the leftovers in the fridge. I asked her if she wanted to watch a movie and we picked out *Mama Mia* which we'd both seen before but enjoyed enough to watch again.

We sat very close together on the couch and sang together during some of the very fun songs. I admit that we didn't make it to the end of the show, but instead made some very harmonious music of our own before falling asleep in each other's arms.

IX

Sometime in the middle of the night I got up and carried a heavily sleeping Holly into the master bedroom. Her five foot six, 110 pound frame seemed to fit perfectly in my arms. She mumbled a groggy thank you after I tucked her into bed before rolling over and going back to sleep. I was wide awake so I went into the kitchen and brewed some coffee. As I sipped I pondered how best to tackle the problem before me. In some ways being a private investigator is analogous to fishing. You just cast about trying different ways to reach your objective and hope something finally hits. I often found it helpful to jot down some notes, so I sat down in front of my computer and typed out some bullets of what I'd heard so far. It still seemed important to try and get a handle on the source of Doug's income. The obvious first step to answering that question was to ask his parents. I also decided that it was worth trying to pin down if the murder had actually taken place where Doug's body was found, or if he had been killed elsewhere and moved. Of course the police were almost certainly working on that same angle. That said, I knew Ben's comment was right on regarding the average person, certainly the average person hanging around the Burnside Bridge, would want nothing to do with the police.

I decided there was no time like the present to start trying to get some answers. I had no desire to wander about the vicinity of Burnside Bridge by myself without some protection so I pulled my stainless .45 Colt and shoulder holster out of the locked drawer I kept it in my desk. I double checked to make sure the clip in the butt was loaded and the second clip was also full. The Colt .45 had long been a standard sidearm for the U.S. military before being replaced by the Beretta M9. I'd had a lot of opportunities to become very adept with the weapon as a Gunners Mate in the Coast Guard and had continued to hone my skills during frequent trips to a nearby firing range. I pulled on the shoulder holster and got a windbreaker out of the closet in the second bedroom. I jotted a quick note to Holly thanking her for a lovely evening and letting her know I might see her before she left in the morning. I set the note on the bedside table pausing for a moment to stroke her cheek and pull back a stray wisp of her golden blonde hair away from her face. Even in deep sleep she had a smile on her face which was one of the many things I loved about her.

I looked at my watch and saw that it was just before 1:00 am. It was probably just about time for the night life downtown to get going. I quietly left the house and locked the door securely behind me.

X

I TOOK A FEW passes in my truck through the Burnside Bridge area on the downtown side of the river to get an idea of how much was going on. I didn't see anything unusual, or more unusual than normal which covered a lot of ground for that area at that time, so found a parking spot just off Burnside in China Town. I made sure to lock my truck and nonchalantly walked down the block and turned on Burnside towards the bridge. There was a fair amount of activity for an early Tuesday morning, but I attributed that partly due to the mild weather.

I passed a group of obviously drunk young men who were loudly discussing the sights they had just seen in a nearby strip club. They were too self absorbed to take any notice of me, for which I was grateful. I had no interest in speaking to them as it was clear that they weren't part of the "local" crowd. I turned and went down the steps to the area below the bridge and crossed the street to the greenway along the river. There was the usual number of decrepit drunks looking for handouts. I debated trying to speak to them, but decided against that for now. It was obvious that they were pretty far gone and I was sure I had no hope of extracting coherent information from them. That was the extent of what I saw on my first walk through. I needed to kill some time so I found a bar that was open and ordered a Power's rocks just to have something in my hands. I took my time with the drink savoring the warmth that spread through my belly. The place was very noisy and I was pretty much unnoticed in the hubbub. Once I finished I paid up and left a good tip just in case I had to return later.

I took another stroll along Burnside pausing once in a while to lean in a doorway and watch the goings on. As I approached a corner a group of three young men came out of the cross street and turned my way. These gentlemen did not look like drunks and were dressed in baggy pants and NFL football jerseys that were far too big for them. I felt a twinge of anxiety as I walked towards them trying not to show any weakness. I'd unzipped my windbreaker when I left the bar and was very glad I'd done so. As we approached each other, I deliberately avoided eye contact and mentally kept my fingers crossed. They seemed to slow down just a bit as we drew alongside each other but I kept on walking and they did too, for which I thanked my lucky stars. I had great faith in the power of crossed fingers or whatever other superstition happened to work at the time.

Nothing eventful happened on that second pass through. I saw nobody I had an interest in speaking to so I went back to the bar I'd been in before and sat on the same bar stool I'd been in not 45 minutes ago. The bar tender asked what I'd have with no sign of ever having seen me before. I thought, "so much for leaving a big tip." I ordered the same and sat back in my chair. I hadn't had time to take more than a couple of sips when a woman pushed her way through the people around the bar and sat down in the open stool beside me. She had black hair that was obviously dyed and bright red lipstick with a sleeveless button down shirt tied off at the waist. Her nice legs were on full display below a very short black leather skirt. At first I thought she was in her late twenties but I looked again and saw hardness around her eyes and mouth and revised my age guesstimate up a decade or so.

She said in what I think she thought was a sultry voice, "Hey honey, weren't you in here just a while ago? I thought you left and was sorry I missed you." Given I'd never seen this woman before I doubted her sincerity, but my grand dad always said you catch more flies with sugar than vinegar so I just replied, "Yep, I was here but I went out for a walk to get out of the noise. Can I buy you a drink?" I asked the last question not entirely willingly but just to avoid any potential fracas.

She batted her eyes at me and said, "I thought you'd never ask," and then turned and hollered down the bar, "Hey Martin, gimme a vodka tonic, will ya?"

The bar tender stoically mixed and set her drink in front of her and said, "That'll be $15 for the two," and looked at me with what I thought was disdain.

Knowing this was perhaps the worst $15 I'd ever spent, I paid without murmur and turned to the woman, gave her a mock toast and said, "Cheers." She responded in kind and took a healthy gulp of her drink. I figured I might as well try and do what I came to do and casually asked her, "Do you hang around down here often?"

She snorted and said, "Yeah, I practically live here. I've never seen you here though. Are you from out of town?" I shook my head and responded, "No, I live here but rarely come downtown. Just out stretching my legs." Trying to strike an offhand tone I continued, "Pretty bad what happened to that guy last night isn't it?" She immediately stiffened, finished off the other half of her drink and said curtly, "Sure, thanks for the drink. I gotta go," and she stood up and made her somewhat wobbly way back through the crowd.

Intrigued by her response, I considered following her through the crowd but decided against that for now. I felt like I was on thin ice and did not want to ruin a chance to get any shreds of information she might have. Based on her comment about spending a lot of time here, I figured I could follow up with her later. I looked at my watch and saw it was just after four o'clock and decided I'd had enough. I put the remainder of my drink down and left the bar without feeling the need to tip Martin.

XI

By the time I got back home it was about four thirty and I was beat. I felt emotionally drained from the desperation I'd seen in some of the faces during my walk downtown and physically grimy from the smoke in the bar. I stripped off my clothes and headed for the shower trying to be as quiet as I could. I turned the water as hot as I could stand it and stood under the stream feeling better every second. I was almost asleep on my feet when I was aware that I was no longer alone. I turned to find that Holly had joined me. She looked beautiful despite it being way before her normal waking up time. We held each other for a time and I felt her calmness and serenity envelope me and I felt whole again.

We stood there for I don't know how long before she looked up at me and said, "I missed you. Can we go back to sleep now?" I smiled down at her and said that sounded like the best idea I'd ever heard. I turned off the water and we toweled each other off and headed for the bed when we were done. I think I was fast asleep before my head hit the pillow.

I awoke feeling much more lively than I had a right to and looked at the clock on the bedside table. It was just before 7:30. I could hear Holly moving around in the kitchen and knew the darling woman was making breakfast. I got up, put on my robe, and headed into the kitchen quietly and stopped, leaned against the wall, and watched Holly moving around humming ABBA songs. She turned and saw me and said, "Hey, good morning, Matt. I hope I didn't wake you. Since you're up, how about some breakfast?"

I told her that sounded great and she poured coffee and handed that to me. She said she had scrambled eggs and bacon ready and told me to pull up a chair. I did so and she was as good as her word. We ate in companionable silence while reading the morning edition of the Oregonian. When she was done she said, "I'm off to work. Are you still planning on trying to meet with the Peterson's?"

I answered by saying, "Yes, I'll give it some time but will call their home at nine or so. I'd guess Mr. Peterson will be at his office, which might be good. I'd prefer to tackle them one at a time. Have a good day at work and I'll call and check in with you later, okay?" She said that sounded fine and gave me a peck on the cheek and headed out the door.

After she left, I topped off my coffee and sat back down at the table to go through the paper in detail. I was pleased to see that the Blazers (Portland's NBA basketball team) had won the night before and was still very much alive in the playoff race. I chuckled at the fishing report which stated that fishing on the Clackamas continued to be very poor. I guess I had the paper to thank for so few people being in my spot the morning before. Finding nothing else illuminating and nothing about the Peterson homicide in the rest of the pages, I folded up the paper and put it in the recycle container.

I had decided not to call the Peterson home until at least 9am, so I had time for a quick swim. I headed to the club. No Monique this morning, which left me feeling a bit put out. I said hello to the front desk person who was there so as not to be a poor sport and headed to my locker. I swam hard for forty-five minutes and quickly showered and got dressed for the day. By the time I was done, it was about nine thirty so I headed to my truck, sat, and dialed the Peterson house. A voice I guessed was Gillian Anderson answered. I identified myself and asked if I could speak to Ms. Peterson. The voice said, "One moment, please" and there was a pause. After a very short wait, a different voice came on the line and identified itself as Eleanor Peterson. She went on to say, "Good morning, Mr. MacKinnon. Have you made any progress yet?"

I said, "Well, not really, but I do have some questions for you, Ms. Peterson. Might I have a moment of your time this morning? I'm sorry for the short notice."

Ms. Peterson said, "Certainly, I'd be happy to answer any questions and please feel free to come over as soon as possible. I do have several appointments starting at about eleven and will be occupied the rest of the day." I said that sounded great and told her I would be right over. As I hung up I wondered what appointments could be so important that they would prevent her from seeing me later on and was glad I did not have to press the point.

It was about ten when I pulled into the driveway and drove beneath the impressive Douglas fir trees again. I parked and walked up to the front door and did not have to wait long after ringing the doorbell before Gillian Anderson opened the door. "Good morning Mr. MacKinnon." She said, "Please follow me." She led me into the same office I'd been in before. There was already a coffee service on the table and Ms. Peterson was sitting in the chair she'd been in the day before. Gillian went through the drill of announcing my presence, asking if she could get us anything, and when told no she left closing the door behind her.

Ms. Peterson was wearing a very becoming business style pants suit with what looked to be a large diamond on a gold necklace with matching earrings. She asked if I would take coffee and I said I would and thanked her. As she poured, I noticed her nails were a different color than the day before and glistened. She obviously had her own ways of dealing with grief. After pouring gracefully, she set the pot down and asked what she could do for me.

I responded, "Ms. Peterson, I hope this question does not offend you, but I feel it is important that I know where your son's money came from." I deliberately did not mention what I learned from Alex because I did not want to put her on the spot. I continued, "It would be helpful if I knew about his business dealings." I noticed that beneath the expertly applied makeup that Ms. Peterson's cheeks blushed. Which emotion she felt, sorrow or anger, I could not tell.

She took a breath and said, "Well, Mr. MacKinnon, I suppose I can understand why you might ask that. The truth is my son did not have what you would call a regular job. I know he thought of himself as an entrepreneur however, and he was working on several potentially lucrative business deals. I doubt very much that any of his associates are implicated in his death."

Thinking I'd already pushed one button, I figured I'd try and go for another and said, "Ms. Peterson did the business dealings you mention include the work your husband does? I believe Alex mentioned your husband is a financial advisor. Was that the same line of work your son was in?"

Ms. Peterson's facial expression answered the question of which emotion I had evoked. It was not sorrow. With a set expression and firm tone she stated, "Mr. MacKinnon, my son's business dealings had nothing to do with my husband's. Doug chose to forge his own way, which I must say I approved of and encouraged. It would have been very easy for him to simply ride his father's coat tails but he chose not to do that."

I wasn't going to let up yet so I continued, "Ms. Peterson did you and your husband provide funds for your son's business? I'm sorry if this is painful for you to describe but you know as well as I do that oftentimes high stakes money dealings can lead to problems. I don't mean to imply that this would be caused by your son. Perhaps he had a jealous competitor or creditor."

My apology seemed to mollify her a bit. She took a sip of coffee before responding, "Yes, I understand. Since you ask, I can tell you that my husband insisted that we establish a trust fund for Doug. It provided him an income that he could live on and some capital with which to fund his endeavors. If you must know this arrangement was a source of some discord in our household. I wanted to be more forthcoming with funds, and could have done so because I've some money of my own, but my husband felt it provided more of a life lesson if Doug had some stable income and had to manage that income." She let out a transparently false laugh and continued, "I doubt very many families are immune to such squabbling and we certainly had our share but we all worked through the issues. It is hard for me to air these details. I regret coming across as defensive."

I noticed the color in her cheeks had subsided and I remarked to myself that Ben's earlier comment that this woman was one cool customer was right on the mark. I did not know whether to admire her or feel sorry for her given the tragedy she was covering. I was brought back from my wandering thoughts by her asking, "Well, Mr. MacKinnon, I think I've been very patient in answering your questions. I think I'd like to ask one of my own, if I may." I said certainly and she continued, "Can you give me a run down on your activities on my behalf since we spoke yesterday?"

I had the distinct impression that this was a deliberate counter to put me on the spot and I gave her credit for turning the tables so neatly. I thanked my lucky stars that I hadn't slept the night away and was gratified to see her reaction when I told her what I'd been up to in the wee hours of the morning. She cleared her throat and said, "I'm gratified to know that you did not come to harm on my behalf, Mr. MacKinnon. I would not have dreamed that you would pursue such a line of investigation. I suppose such activities are common place for someone in your line of work though. Can you tell me what your intentions are?"

I told her I hadn't given up on finding someone who might have seen something the night of her son's death. I also mentioned that I hoped to continue to trace down business associates since Doug had told Alex that he had business to conduct before dropping her off. She nodded and asked me to provide reports as I learned anything and then pointedly looked at her watch. I took my cue, put down my cup, and stood saying that I could show myself out. I did so, shutting the door firmly behind me. I admit to feeling a tad devious by not mentioning to Ms. Peterson that I intended to follow up on Doug's business dealings by speaking to her husband. I consoled myself by deciding the woman probably played cards and would understand the concept of keeping one's cards close to the chest.

XII

I DROVE BACK DOWN the driveway debating how best to secure a meeting with Doug's father and decided the most direct way was to just call. I had Alex's cell number and dialed it. She answered on the third ring and said hello and asked me what was up. I asked her if she had Mr. Peterson's cell or work number and she said, "no, but the company name is Unlimited Horizons Investing." I thanked her and told her I hope she was doing okay. She said she was doing just fine and asked when the three of us could get together. I told her anytime was a-okay by me and that she and Holly should just plan something. With that we hung up and I called directory assistance and got the number for Peterson's office.

I dialed the number and a very efficient sounding woman said, "Unlimited Horizons Investing, this is Megan. How may I help you?" I answered, "Hello, Megan, my name is Matt MacKinnon and I would like to speak to Mr. Peterson." Megan told me that Peterson was in a meeting with a client. She asked me what the nature of the call was. I said, "I'm working on a private matter on behalf of Mr. Peterson's wife. I'm sorry I can't say any more than that." Without missing a beat she asked if she could have my number. I gave it to her and she said someone would return my call as soon as possible. I hung up trying not to feel frustrated that I could not have my get together with Peterson right away.

I was left with time on my hands and I wondered how best to proceed. I wasn't far from my house so I decided to head there and have some lunch. I am a big leftover fan and there was some stroganoff calling my name. I pulled into the driveway, parked and headed inside. I hit the fridge first and got the stroganoff container out and into the microwave for a couple of minutes. While that was heating up I checked my message machine and noticed the light was blinking. I hit play and was astounded to hear Gillian Anderson's voice say, "Mr. MacKinnon, this is Gillian Anderson phoning. This is very irregular but I would like to speak to you as soon as possible. My personal cell number is 503-236-2170 and you can call at any time." There was a pause and then she continued in a confused tone, "Mr. MacKinnon, my employer does not know I am calling and I'd like to keep it that way if possible. Thank you for your consideration." With that the message ended. Of course only then did I remember Gillian's red, puffy eyes. I knew she had been crying just before I had met her the day before.

I dialed the number she left in her message and a voice I recognized as hers answered after a couple of rings. I identified myself and she said, "Thank you for returning my call, Mr. MacKinnon. Are you able to meet me somewhere? I'd like to speak to you about Doug's death." She paused but continued with a catch in her voice, "Ms. Peterson is at a luncheon event with several friends and they will be meeting for some time. I prefer not to speak over the phone."

I responded, "Yes, of course, I can meet wherever you like. Tell me where you are and we can pick a spot near there." She said, "The luncheon is at the Embassy Suites downtown. Can we meet at Kincaid's? I'll be at a table in the back corner of the bar." Kincaid's is the restaurant in the same building as the Embassy Suites downtown. I told her I could be there within ten minutes and we hung up.

I needed to move fast so I left quickly, not without a look of longing at the microwave that had beeped while I was on the phone, and drove downtown. Parking can be a challenge in downtown Portland but I managed to find a spot very close to the Embassy Suites building. I walked in through the Kincaid's entrance on 3rd Avenue and turned into the bar area and headed towards the back. The place was, as usual, quite busy but I saw Gillian Anderson at a quiet table away from the hustle and bustle. She looked strained and as I walked up I smiled at her and stuck out my hand. She shook it somewhat hesitantly. She said, "Thank you for coming so promptly Mr. MacKinnon. I don't have much time but I have to talk to someone and didn't know where else to turn." I said, "Ms. Anderson, let's not stand on ceremony. Please call me

Matt." She responded with a wan smile and said, "In that case please call me Gillian." At that moment the waitress came up and asked if she could bring us anything. I ordered a local porter from the tap and Gillian ordered a Glenfiddich rocks. We sat in silence while waiting for our drinks to arrive and I could see her trying to compose herself. As soon as our drinks were deposited before us and the waitress had moved away I said, "Okay, Gillian, everything is going to be fine. Just relax and take your time."

She took a sip of her Scotch, put her glass down, and said, "I have to tell you that if Ms. Peterson knew I was speaking to you like this I would certainly be fired. She is a very hard nosed woman. If I were fired that might come as a relief to me because I have come to despise her loathsome husband." She paused to take another pull on her drink and continued, "Unfortunately I don't have another source of income lined up and can't afford to just quit." I could see her features relax and knew that the combination of alcohol and getting the words out was therapeutic.

I said, "Gillian, I don't know Ms. Peterson well and don't know Mr. Peterson at all, but I get a strong feeling that they are very cold people. I don't know if I admire or pity Ms. Peterson for the way she is dealing with her son's death. Has she just not come to terms with that?"

She looked at me and shook her head, "Matt, I don't think either of those people truly loved their son. I have been with Ms. Peterson for two years and I have concluded Doug was just a pawn in a never ending power struggle between the two of them." At this point her eyes filled with tears. I gave her time to regain her composure. She did so, looked at me, and said, "What I have to tell you is that over the course of my time with the Peterson's, I found myself falling in love with Doug. It was a hopeless passion, but he was aware of my feelings. Because of that he confided in me and, if I look at the situation dispassionately, took advantage of me. I was willing to do anything for him and he asked me to loan him money which I did. Doug hated his father but despite that struggled desperately to impress him. Doug always was trying various high risk get rich quick schemes. On top of that I think he had a serious gambling problem. What I really wanted to tell you is that several months ago Doug stopped asking me for loans. I asked him about that and he told me he had finally convinced his father to take him seriously and that his father had been providing him money. I asked him how he had changed his father's opinion and he just smirked and said it didn't matter. His tone when he told me that was very cold and it was clear there hadn't been reconciliation."

We both finished our drinks and I looked at Gillian inquisitively and she nodded. I caught the waitress's eye and made the universal "another round" gesture. She nodded, and I turned back to Gillian and said, "Gillian, I can certainly understand why you are so upset. I'm sorry for your troubles. Are you aware of the trust fund the Peterson's created for Doug? If yes, do you think that was what Doug was speaking of when he said his father had started providing some money?" I stopped to allow the waitress to set the second round of drinks in front of us. She asked if there would be anything else and I grinned at her and said no thanks. She grinned back and left.

Gillian said, "Yes, I knew about the trust fund. I'm not sure when it was set up but it was long before the time I'm talking about. I had the impression that Doug's father had agreed to provide money in addition to the income Doug derived from the fund."

I gave her a puzzled look and said, "That is odd. When I spoke to Ms. Peterson she told me that she had always wanted to give Doug more money than her husband did and it was Doug's father who insisted on establishing the fund. I wonder if Ms. Peterson is aware that her husband had a change of heart." Gillian shook her head and said, "I very much doubt it. She never said anything about it."

We sat in quiet reflection for a few moments nursing our drinks. After a time she said, "Matt, I wasn't around very often when Mr. and Mrs. Peterson were together but I had a sense that their relationship was very strained. I also got the feeling that Mr. Peterson was under more stress than normal. As you know he is a partner in an investment firm. I wonder if his firm was in some sort of trouble." She paused and said, "This may sound out of place but I was present during a few of the times your friend Alex was at the Peterson home for social occasions. I have to say that as much as I wanted to dislike her because she had Doug's affection; I couldn't because she was such a kind person. I think she was aware of my feelings and it seemed she took pains to alleviate awkwardness. I hope she is doing well?"

I nodded at her and said, "Alex is a very kind person and I consider her a close friend. She is doing as well as can be expected." I refrained from mentioning Alex's comment that she was trying to find a way to break it off with Doug. At that moment my cell phone rang and I excused myself and answered it. It was Megan at Unlimited Horizons letting me know Mr. Peterson was free and could speak to me now. I said that would be great, and she asked me to hold while she patched him through. I pushed the mute button and quickly told Gillian who was on the line and asked her if she could wait, she nodded and I thanked her. Just then a very brusque voice said, "This is Earl Peterson. I understand from my receptionist that you are working on something for my wife. What is this about?"

"Mr. Peterson, I am a private investigator and your wife has engaged me to look into the death of your son. I have some questions I'd like to ask you but I prefer not to do so over the phone. May I have an appointment to meet with you?"

There was a long pause before he replied, "I have a very busy afternoon lined up MacKinnon. I have no idea what you can do that the police cannot and I can't believe my wife hired you. I'll go through with this farce if only to humor my wife. I can make some time at four o'clock." I thanked him, told him that would be fine, and he tersely gave me his office address and abruptly hung up.

I put my phone away and said to Gillian, "Well, I'm sure you gathered from my side of the conversation that I'm meeting with Mr. Peterson. He was not happy and is only reluctantly going along. I doubt I'm in for a very pleasant interview. Would you care for another?" Gillian shook her head no and thanked me for listening to her. She continued, "I feel much better Matt. I should get back to the event and check in with Ms. Peterson." I thanked her for her confidence and gave her my card and wrote my cell phone number on the back. I asked her if she would give me a call if she thought of anything that might help in my investigation. She promised she would. I told her I would get the drinks and she thanked me and left the bar and went through the door into the hotel lobby.

The porter was very good and I had time on my hands so I decided to sit back down and finish the beer. By this time the lunch time crowd had mostly left and the waitress came over and we chatted a bit. She was a very happy person and I found myself wishing there were more people like her and Holly in the world.

XIII

I GOT BACK TO my truck just as the parking meter was turning over to zero. I'm sure I ruined the day for the parking enforcement officer who had his ticket book in his hand and had been waiting for the last few seconds to tick by. I told him "better luck next time amigo," and waved a cheerful farewell as I pulled away from the curb and left him scowling in my rear view mirror. I had a couple of hours until my meeting with Peterson so I decided to give Ben Canfield a call. I hadn't had any lunch while chatting with Gillian and could feel the Porters I'd consumed on an empty stomach. Hoping Ben was feeling up for lunch as well I punched in his number and he answered right away. "Hey, Matt, I just wrapped up some interviews with some people the blues brought in from Burnside. I'm hoping that you've got something for me besides a lunch invitation, those interviews were utterly futile."

I responded, "Well, Ben, I'm not sure if I've got anything for you, but I could do with some lunch. How about we meet at Dan and Louis's?" This was a favorite oyster bar spot in downtown that had great seafood at reasonable prices. He quickly agreed and we hung up. I was only a couple of blocks away so beat him there and had no problem getting a table. We'd met there several times since we worked together a few months past, so I knew he was partial to the Commissioner Stew which was loaded with oysters, Dungeness crab, and bay shrimp. I placed an order for two of the same. He came in just in time to have a big bowl of the savory stew plunked down in front of him.

Ben didn't waste any words, but put a napkin in his lap and spooned up a first bite. He sighed and said, "That just made up for my entire wasted morning. Just what the doctor ordered, thanks. What have you been up to?"

I hadn't waited to dig in myself so had to pause to swallow before answering, "I had a very interesting chat with Gillian Anderson, Mrs. Peterson's personal assistant." He nodded and I continued, "She phoned and left a message this morning after I met with her boss. I called her back and we met at Kincaid's, in fact I just left her there about twenty minutes ago. I have to say she did not want this conversation to be known to her employer."

Ben shrugged and said, "Sure, you know I'll do my best, but if push comes to shove and it'll help lock down a case, she may have to testify."

I said I understood and was sure she would as well. I continued, "Well, turns out Mr. Peterson the father had started providing cash to Doug in addition to what was provided under the terms of a trust fund the Petersons had set up for their son. This was a very recent development and Gillian said it was not due to any reconciliation. She also said that Mr. Peterson senior had seemed more than usually tense. She speculated that it might be due to business woes. It doesn't seem like these two stories quite jive. Final tidbit is Gillian did not think Doug's mother was aware of the cash on the side. Why would Peterson start giving the kid more money if the business was hurting?"

Ben looked intrigued and said, "Well, the trust fund came out during our interview with the father. I find it interesting that the additional cash did not come up during that same conversation."

He paused so I continued, "I've got a meet set up with him at four this afternoon. Needless to say he was less than enthusiastic about that and he said he was going along just to humor his wife."

We looked at each other and at the same time began to shake our heads. He said, "I think you and I are thinking the same thing. It just doesn't seem that those two have a very simpatico relationship. If anything, my sense is they'd not agree to do something the other wanted just out of spite." I nodded and he said, "I can't help but wonder if he's meeting with you just to pick your brain and find out what you know and are guessing."

I took up the thought, "I'm wondering if I should hit him with the question about the cash he had been providing his son on the side. On the other hand it might be worth holding out on that and see where he goes? What do you think?"

Ben nodded and said, "Either one of those angles could have merit for sure. Another question is if we should sound out the wife and see what her reaction is to that news." At that moment Ben's phone rang, he pulled it out of his jacket pocket and said, "Yeah, Dave, what's up?" He listened to the voice on the other end and his eyebrows went up towards his hairline. "Heck, I'm not three blocks from there. I'll be there in a flash." He hung up his phone and said, "You're not going to believe this. Gillian Anderson was just shot in a parking garage just a couple of blocks from here. She's in transit to Good Sam and was alive but in very tough shape. I need to meet Dave there as soon as possible. Can you get this?" He pointed at the bill and I nodded yes. Over his shoulder as he walked away, Ben said "There is something really rotten going on here, Matt. Be very careful."

I paid the check, walked out of the restaurant, and headed down the sidewalk towards my truck. No parking attendant this time. I looked at my watch and saw that I still had plenty of time before my interview with Peterson. I had the sudden urge to see if Mrs. Peterson had allowed her lunch function to be interrupted by something as mundane as the shooting of her personal assistant. I was only two blocks from the Embassy so I plugged more change in the parking meter and strode off.

I entered the impressive lobby of the hotel and looked for an announcement board for functions taking place in the various meeting rooms. There were several choices but I put high odds that the one I was looking for was the Washington Park Zoo Charity Foundation. I noted that it was in the Fireside Room on the Mezzanine level and was scheduled to go from noon to four. As I jogged up the wide stairs I worked out the odds that Ms. Peterson was still in the meeting. If the death of an only son didn't prompt a cancelation, I figured the shooting of a personal assistant wouldn't merit much action. Fortunately I was not faced with closed doors and I was able to peek in.

Sure enough, she was there at a round table with four other women ranging in age from what I guessed to be late 20s to late 50s. There were several other tables that were all filled with a mixture of well dressed people of both genders. A youngish man in an expensive suit was working his way through a Power Point presentation that seemed to center around housing for chimpanzees. I listened for a few moments hoping Ms. Peterson would spot me and excuse herself and come out to see what I was doing there. I had no doubt that she noticed me standing in the doorway as she was situated such that she could see me with a small turn of her head, but she seemed riveted by the Habitat For Humanity's Closest Cousin spiel.

I waited patiently until the suit had finished and took advantage of the scattered applause to enter the room and walk over to Ms. Peterson. I kneeled down beside her so as to be discreet as possible. She turned to me with what seemed like feigned surprise and whispered, "Mr. MacKinnon, what in the world are you doing here? I thought I had made it clear that I was unavailable this afternoon?"

I nodded and whispered back, "I'm sorry to intrude, Ms. Peterson, but I have some bad news I thought you should know. Ms. Anderson was just shot in the parking garage across the street. She is on her way to Good Samaritan right now and I understand she is in critical condition."

As I spoke Ms. Peterson's faced drained of color and she reached for a glass of ice water and took a long drink as if hoping it was something far stronger. She put her glass down and started to speak but choked off what she had been about to say. During our interchange her dining companions had studiously avoided looking in our direction but it was obvious they were straining to hear our comments. I could also see curious glances being directed our way from people at other tables. An older, well dressed, man had taken over the lectern from the chimpanzee man and was glaring in our direction as if mortally offended by my entrance.

It was obvious that Ms. Peterson was struggling with what to do so I decided to let her off the hook by leaning in close and quietly saying, "I realize this is a shock. I'll let you be and give you some time to decide what to do. I'll wait outside for a bit if you decide to take a break from your luncheon, but I do have an appointment I have to leave for soon." With that I stood up and said in my most urbane manner, "Sorry to disrupt your lunch, ladies. Long live Curious George." The youngest of the group covered a snort of laughter by coughing into her napkin. The other women glared at me and I turned on my heel and walked away.

I waited just outside the room on the Mezzanine landing and pulled a quarter out of my pocket. I gave it a flip and thought to myself, tails she comes out, and it turned up heads. Because of that I did not wait very long but I didn't think I needed the coin to tell me Ms. Peterson wasn't about to leave her social event for something as trivial as the shooting of someone in her employ.

XIV

PETERSON'S OFFICE WAS ONLY a few blocks away from the Embassy Suites so I topped off the parking meter and walked up the hill. I wanted to check on Gillian Anderson so I called up Ben. He answered, I asked how Gillian was, and he said she was still in surgery but the initial report was that she would make it. I thanked him and we hung up. I decided I wanted to send some flowers to Gillian so she had something cheerful to look at when she came out of surgery. Fortunately I had the number of my favorite florist saved in my contact list. I made a quick call and set up for a delivery to the hospital with the owner. By this time I had reached the address for Unlimited Horizons and I stopped in front of the impressive building and looked at my watch. Just before my appointed time so I walked on into the foyer and headed for the elevator. I pushed the appropriate buttons and stepped out when the doors opened on the correct floor. It was a pretty snazzy setup but I figured it had to be to attract the kind of well heeled clients such a firm made most of their money on.

I stepped through the shining glass door marked Unlimited Horizons Investing and approached the reception desk. Seated behind the glass top desk was a very attractive young woman wearing a conservative business skirt and matching jacket. I saw the name tag on the desk read Megan, so deduced this was the woman I'd spoken to on the phone earlier. Megan was on the phone, but she smiled in my direction as I walked up and said into the blue tooth device clipped to her ear, "Mrs. Logan, I will have Mr. Peterson phone you as soon as he is available.

Have a good afternoon." With that she pushed a very small button on the earpiece and said to me, "Hello, are you Mr. MacKinnon?"

I smiled back at her and said, "Yes, I am, Megan. Is Mr. Peterson available?" She nodded, stood up, and said, "Yes, he is expecting you and asked me to walk you in right away. He has a meeting at 4:20 so your visit will have to be relatively brief. Please follow me." She turned and walked away and I was very happy to do just that. She reached a dark wooden door down a short carpeted hallway, knocked, and entered when a muffled voice answered. As she stepped in she said, "Mr. MacKinnon is here, Mr. Peterson." She gestured me to pass by her and I did so catching a whiff of a very nice perfume as I did so. I thanked her as she left closing the door behind her.

The man on the other side of the desk typified what I considered the "Wall Street power broker" look. He looked very fit and wore an expensive dark suit, red stripped power tie, white shirt, and glossy black wing tips. The look did not end with the clothes; it was obvious that his silver colored hair had been very recently expertly cut. The big corner office fit the look with high glass windows looking out across the river with Mount Hood in the distant background, mahogany cushioned chairs, and the large mahogany desk behind which he sat. I knew in a moment that offering to shake hands was out of the question so I merely stood there waiting for him to speak.

He seemed content to wait me out for a few moments but finally gestured a manicured hand at one of the chairs, "I'm sure Megan told you I have another meeting in a very short time," he said, "You told me on the phone you had some questions. Before we get to those may I see your credentials?"

I pulled the leather bifold case that held my private investigator license and concealed handgun license out of my back pocket and handed it across to him before settling into one of the chairs across the desk from him. He took it and gave it a perfunctory glance before sliding it back across the desk. He stated rather coolly, "Well, you seem to be legitimate. What did you have in mind for questions?"

As I returned my case to my pocket I said, "Thank you for taking a few moments of your time to see me, Mr. Peterson. I did speak with your wife this morning and she was unable to fill in some details on your son's business dealings for me. She did mention that the two of you had established a trust fund for Doug from which he gleaned a stable income. Am I correct in thinking you were the one who provided the initial investment and determined the details of the trust?"

He looked at me and said, "Of course I set up the trust, that is what I do for a living and I live very well. The trust was set up to provide my son with a decent income that was enough for him to live a modest life style and, if invested wisely, potentially to live better than that."

I nodded and said, "That seems very generous, Mr. Peterson. I understand from Mrs. Peterson that your son chose not to follow in your footsteps in the investment advisor business. She was unable to tell me what line of business your son did chose though. I believe that it is worth investigating what business dealings your son did have; perhaps he made some enemies or some bad investments with the wrong people. Forgive me for speaking frankly."

Peterson's eyes had hardened during my question and he spoke more severely as he answered, "Mr. MacKinnon, you are correct that my son did not choose to work in this business and he certainly did not follow in my footsteps. I made every effort to bring him along and afforded him every opportunity to make a good career in the company my partner and I built. Why he chose not to take advantage of those opportunities is unknown to me, but I doubt very much that what work he did do had anything to do with his death. I actually don't know what he had going, nothing very worthwhile as far as I can tell, and I do not know with whom he associated."

I could sense this conversation was going nowhere so I decided to try and shake him up a bit. I straightened in my chair and asked, "Mr. Peterson, I understand that you and your wife disagreed on how much support to provide your son. What I don't understand is why you changed your mind and began providing additional financial support outside the terms of the trust a few months ago. Did you and your wife reach an agreement on a compromise after all?"

I could see his jaw clench and for a moment I thought he was going to get up, walk around the desk, and take a slug at me, but instead he glanced at his watch and said, "I'm afraid your time is up MacKinnon. I can't think of anything I can tell you to help you complete the task my wife hired you to do. In my opinion she was misguided to not leave the matter to the professionals in the police department. Good day."

I'd obviously struck the nerve I'd hoped to and was very reluctant to let it go but it was obvious that he was going to clam up and I would get nothing else. I stood up and said, "Mr. Peterson, I hope you understand my sole intent is to bring your son's killer to justice. I don't wish to seem impertinent but I have to disagree with you. I believe the details of your son's finances may shed some light on his death. You more than anyone can understand the power of money and what people will do to get it. I hope you reconsider your decision to not speak more freely. Here is my card. Feel free to call at any time. Thank you for your time." With that I turned and walked out of the office and back down the hall. Megan was on the phone speaking into her ear piece but she smiled and watched me walk down the hall and past her desk. I waved goodbye to her and she returned the gesture.

XV

I WALKED BACK DOWNTOWN towards my truck and thought about my all too brief conversation with Peterson. I didn't think I could have handled it in a way to get more information from him but I couldn't help but chide myself for turning him off so quickly. Even though I'd learned nothing definitive I thought I'd give Ben a call and let him know how my interview went. I was also concerned about Gillian and I was sure Ben was still at the hospital. He answered his cell on the second ring and said, "Hey Matt, are you already done with your chat with Peterson?"

I responded, "Unfortunately, yes, Ben, probably the shortest interview I've ever had. I did spring the cash on the side question on him and his response was an immediate shutdown. There's definitely something there but I'm not going to get it from him. Maybe you can drag something out of him by flashing your badge and throwing your office around a bit?"

Ben said, "Well, it's probably worth a shot. I'm certainly not getting anywhere on any of my other leads. I obviously don't have enough to go to a judge and get a warrant for bank records so I'm going to have to try and bluff a bit. A guy like that is probably secure enough not to fall for such a stunt, but I'll cross my fingers."

I changed tack on him and asked how Gillian was. He answered, "She's still in surgery Matt. I've checked with the doctors and they say it might be a while. I'm going to hang around here until I hear something definitive. You want me to call when there's a change?" I told him that would be great and we exchanged goodbyes and hung up. I glanced at my watch and saw it was just about five which is when Holly usually called it a day. I dialed her number and she picked up and said, "Hey Matt, I'm just headed out the door. How was your day?"

I responded by saying, "Well, Holly, it was a doozy, I can tell you that. How about I fill you in over dinner?" I had debated whether to tell her about Gillian Anderson but had decided to do so in person. She said that she was headed to the club to take Alex on in racquetball, something they frequently did as both women are very good players, but she was happy to get together afterwards. I said, "What do you think about me grilling up some steaks for dinner? You could ask Alex if she wants to join us if you like." Holly loved it when I grilled. Sometimes I think it is the main reason she sticks with me. I had an ulterior motive in asking Alex to join us. I wanted to let her know what happened to Gillian face to face as I knew the news would be a shock. As expected Holly agreed to my proposal and asked me to hold on while she checked with Alex. There was a pause and she came back on and she said Alex would love to join us. We settled on the two of them just showing up when there were done playing racquetball. Just before she hung up, she casually announced, "Matt, I've told Alex how good you are with a grill. She is expecting perfection! Bye."

I smiled because I knew Holly was trying to make me sweat. She knew I took great pride in my grill techniques and couldn't help ribbing me whenever the chance arose. I reached my truck as I put my phone away and drove away from the curb wondering whether to sprinkle hickory chips on the coals or go with a secret spray that originated at a very good steak house called the Channel Club in Sitka, Alaska. I'd eaten at the Channel Club while in Sitka for a fishing trip with my best friend's brother-in-law who had lived there for years and gotten to know the owner of the place very well. Sometimes such connections are very nice to have.

XVI

I STOPPED AT THE grocery store on the way home and picked out three dandy looking rib eyes. I knew my fridge was almost empty so I also picked up some asparagus and spinach salad fixings. My last stop was at a nearby liquor store where I found a couple of bottles of pinot noir from a popular Willamette Valley vineyard on sale that would go well with dinner. Feeling very much up to Holly's not so subtle challenge, I headed home.

After turning on some 3 Doors Down, *Away From the Sun*, I headed to the kitchen. I'd decided on the secret Channel Club spray, so I put the steaks on a platter and applied the spray so they could marinate a bit. I also added a bit of fresh ground garlic just for a little extra pizzazz. With that done I checked on the appetizer. Discovering Holly and I had made a big dent in the smoked steelhead dip I whipped up some more just to be sure I didn't run out before the women showed up. I opened one of the pinots to let it breathe and turned my attention to the salad. I washed a bunch of spinach and put it in a big wooden salad bowl. I added thinly sliced purple onions, mandarin oranges, cut hard boiled eggs, and crumbled bacon left over from breakfast. The asparagus was next. I trimmed it and put it in a steamer in a saucepan with a lid and set it on the stove.

Dinner being very much under control, I headed back for a quick shower. Wearing clean clothes and feeling very refreshed I was more than ready for a glass of wine and smoked fish dip. I was halfway through the first glass when there was a knock on the door. Holly and Alex came on up the stairs without waiting to be let in. Both women looked fantastic with the high color that comes from a good work out. They were dressed very casually wearing blue jeans and T-shirts, Holly in an Oregon State shirt and Alex in a University of Oregon shirt (which demonstrated their playful competition was not reserved for the racquetball court) with their hair in pony tails. The three of us exchanged hello hugs and I poured them some wine. Neither of them waited for an invitation to partake in the bagel crisps and dip and I asked them if they wanted to sit out on the deck before it cooled off too much. They were agreeable and we picked up the food and wine and headed outside. I fired up the grill and waited until it was very hot. I had been debating with myself on when to broach the news of Gillian's shooting, but decided to wait until after dinner.

Once the grill was hot, I plopped on the rib eyes and heard the gratifying sizzle that always made my mouth water. I excused myself from the ladies happy conversation; they were both critiquing each other's games and needling the other about certain poor shots. I stepped inside and turned the heat on under the asparagus and dressed the salad with a balsamic vinaigrette dressing I knew they both enjoyed. Fortunately for me the ladies preferred their steaks the same way I did, medium rare, so I turned them all at the same time and applied another dose of spray and garlic. I noticed a couple of empty glasses so topped them off without being asked and was rewarded with two very nice smiles in return.

It was a pleasant evening so when there was a break in the conversation, I asked if they wanted to stick to the out of doors. They both readily agreed and asked if they could help. I told them "no, thanks" and went inside to get plates, silverware, napkins, and the salad. I checked the asparagus and it was just done so turned off the heat, added a pat of butter, a few sprinkles of parmesan cheese, and some lemon juice. Hands full, I headed back to the deck and laid everything out on the red cedar picnic table I'd made a few years earlier. I went back inside for one last load, opening the second bottle of wine to boot, and stepped out and called the ladies to the table. As they complied I turned off the grill and removed the steaks and brought over the platter. I was gratified by their "ohhhs" and "ahhhs". We busily passed things until our plates were full and applied ourselves with gusto.

The three of us exchanged idle chit chat while we ate. Once we were done, both women pronounced dinner a smashing success and toasted my culinary triumph. I took a mock bow and stood up to start gathering plates to take inside. I was promptly informed that I should sit down and digest in peace, the cleanup was the least they could do. And that they did very efficiently. Once clean up was done, I offered Tillamook vanilla ice cream with Mrs. Richardson's fudge. We all decided we had room for one scoop. We sat down at the dining room table with dessert and I cleared my throat and said, "I've been waiting for the right time to tell you both some bad news. Sorry to ruin the evening, but Gillian Anderson was shot in a parking garage just after lunch this afternoon. She is expected to make it, but was in surgery when I last spoke to Ben Canfield. I am expecting him to call with an update."

Holly and Alex responded as expected, expressing sorrow and dismay. Alex put her head in her hands and said, "I always felt so badly for Gillian having to work in that household. She seems like such a nice woman and had to put up with so much from a very demanding employer. She and Doug were very close." With that she looked up and gave me a look that told me she knew just how close they had been.

I said, "Again, I'm so sorry I had to break this to you both, but I didn't want you to just hear it over the news. I hope you understand why I waited, there really isn't a good time to say something like this." Both women nodded in agreement and said they understood. At that moment my cell phone rang and I walked over to where I had set it on the counter and noticed Ben's name in the caller ID. I looked back at Holly and Alex and told them, "Excuse me if I take this call. It is Ben Canfield." I popped open the phone to answer the call and said, "Hi, Ben. What news?"

Ben answered, "Hi, Matt. Well, Ms. Anderson is out of surgery and is awake but of course very groggy. I spoke to the surgeon and learned that the bullet entered her left shoulder and narrowly missed doing almost certainly fatal damage. We collected the bullet as evidence and it is being processed now. It looked like a smaller caliber slug, maybe a .32, and it did not pass all the way through. The doc said that her prognosis is good. She is going to be sedated for most of the night probably, but Dave and I are going to take shifts hanging around just in case she gets coherent enough to make a statement."

I asked, "Ben, has Mrs. Peterson made an appearance?" and he said, "Nope, but there is a very large floral arrangement with a card from her. Just so you know the arrangement you sent is also here and in her room.

I'm sure she'll appreciate your gesture. If you're wondering whether or not to come for a visit, I'd suggest you don't. Even if she does come to, Dave or I will be taking her statement and I bet that would be pushing it."

I thanked him for the advice and told him to get what sleep he could, knowing that was futile. We signed off, and I put my phone back down on the counter. I turned back to the table and rejoined Holly and Alex and relayed Ben's side of the conversation. Holly asked what I intended to do. I told her I was headed back down to Burnside to see if I could scare up someone who had seen anything the night Doug had been killed. Both women expressed their concern for that plan and I told them I'd be extremely careful and go down there armed. Holly asked if she could go with me, but I told her in very unequivocal terms "absolutely not". Knowing from my tone that I would not change my mind or back down, she said, "Well, if you are getting up at one o'clock, you'd better try and get a bit of shut eye since you had such a long night last night. It is time to break this party up, Alex."

I reluctantly agreed and thanked them for their consideration and they got up to go. I walked them down the stairs and Alex turned and gave me a hug goodbye before going out the door. Holly paused and then gave me a hug of her own with a quick kiss which I returned. She made me promise to call her whatever time I got back home so she would know I was okay. I agreed to her demand, recognizing the tone in her voice didn't brook compromise. I watched them get into Holly's car. They had driven to my house together, and they drove away. Once they were gone, I turned back inside and walked upstairs to my bedroom where I took off my clothes and got in bed. I set my alarm for 12:30. I tossed and turned for some time before finally dropping off.

XVII

I WAS DEEP IN a dream that involved Holly, a beach, and not much else when the alarm went off with a clamor that utterly wrecked the dream. I very reluctantly reached over and turned it off, rolled to my feet, and headed to the bathroom. After splashing cold water on my face and brushing my teeth, I padded into the kitchen and got a pot of coffee going before heading back to the bedroom to get dressed. I put on a pair of jeans, a black polo shirt, and tennis shoes and headed back to the kitchen.

When I walked into the kitchen the coffee was done so I poured a cup and took it to the desk where my computer was. I brought my case notes up to date in the log I maintained and pondered about what I intended to do and if it made any sense at all. Deciding it was still worth one more attempt to find a witness to the events in the Burnside Bridge area the night Doug was killed, I finished off my coffee and put the cup in the sink. I retrieved my stainless .45 Colt out of the locked drawer in my desk and donned the shoulder holster. I pulled the handgun out of the holster and cracked open the slide to make sure a round wasn't in the chamber and then closed the action and checked the two magazines. Satisfied that I was suitably armed, I headed downstairs where I grabbed a windbreaker out of the landing closet before stepping outside and locking the door behind me.

I did the same drive through the Burnside area as I had done the night before and noticed it was just as busy as the night before. I parked in the same spot as I had only 24 hours earlier, thinking it seemed like much more time had passed than that. I went ahead and pulled the .45

out, chambered a round and put the firearm back in the holster after double checking to ensure the safety was engaged and the hammer down. Once again I locked my truck and walked down to Burnside Street and took a left towards the bridge.

I saw a few familiar faces from the night before but did not see anyone I felt like speaking to on my first pass through the area on the street adjacent to where the bridge angled up to cross the river. I decided to head down to the area below the bridge along Naito Parkway that runs right along the greenway beside the river.

As I crossed the street I noticed in the dim light from street lights a woman standing near a tree in the greenway. I walked towards her and smiled hello and asked her how she was doing. She looked pathetically young closer up and had a dull expression on her face. She offered up an obviously false smile and asked, "Hey, are you looking for some fun mister?" I responded by saying, "Not really, but I am willing to pay for some of your time if I can ask you some questions." She took a few steps backwards and nervously said, "Hey, I don't want any trouble and didn't do anything. Just leave me alone, okay?"

I put my hands up and said earnestly, "Look, I am not a cop and I don't want any trouble myself. I'm not joking around when I say I'm willing to just pay you for some time to talk. Come on, it has got to be easier than what I suspect you normally do. I'm not a bad guy and I won't hurt you." I saw her eyes look behind me to my left and I turned in time to see a guy trot across the street towards me. I had passed right by him without noticing him and realized he must have been hanging out in the deep shadows below the bridge.

As he approached I heard a click and saw the glimmer of a knife in his right hand. As he drew near he said, "What the hell are you doing hassling my girl here man? Why don't you just get the hell out of here?" As he drew nearer I could see the tough words were coming from young black man who seemed barely older than the woman. He had a medium build and was dressed in very raggedy jeans with a t-shirt and a jean jacket with ratty looking tennis shoes.

I pushed open my wind breaker and let him see the gun beneath my arm. I pointedly said, "I'd take odds you can't get to me with your knife before I pull this and plug you. I don't want to do that and I doubt very much you really want to use the knife. Tell you what, why don't we just calm down here and talk for a couple of minutes? As I told your friend,

I'm not looking for trouble. I just want to talk." As I spoke, he had come to a stop and looked at me as if I'd just sprouted horns and a tail. I noticed that he had the same pathetic, helpless look the young woman did. I took advantage of having the initiative to say, "I don't even want the knife, just put it away and let's talk. My name is Matt. If it makes you feel better, we could get off the street and get some food. Food's on me and I'll give you forty bucks for your time. Come on, think about it. That's a hell of a lot better than working the street." As I spoke I had moved so I could see both of them without having to swivel my head as much. At the mention of food, I thought I saw the girl swallow and look hopeful and I suspected I'd stuck a cord with her at least.

My suspicions were confirmed when she said, "Come on, Joe, I don't know what his game is, but we can always bolt if he turns psycho on us." I noticed she was dressed in cut off shorts, a halter top, with an unzipped black leather jacket with fringe along the underside of both arms.

I could see the guy was struggling with indecision so I just said, "Hey, I'm going to walk to the burger place up Burnside. If you want to take me up on my offer follow when you want to. If you don't then so be it, but that's up to you. I promise I'm not going to cause you any trouble and I am not a cop. I'll wait half an hour and then bag it if you don't show." I knew I was taking a big chance that I was completely wasting my time, but I had a hunch that these two kids spent a lot of time in the shadows and might have seen something that I'd find worth my time. If nothing else, I was doing them a temporary good turn by giving them some food in safer circumstances than it seemed they were used to. I found their situation unspeakably sad and couldn't help but wonder what their story was.

I kept my hands out and walked around the guy and when I was far enough away I turned on my heel and headed back across the street. I did not look back, but when I walked up the steps that led back up to the upper level of Burnside I could see the two of them slowly trailing behind me. I turned right when I got to the top of the steps and headed up the street to a burger joint that was open late. After walking a couple of blocks I could not help but turn slightly so I could see behind me and there they were seemingly talking earnestly but far enough away that I could not catch their words. Of course I did not blame them for being suspicious, I'd no doubt they had met some pretty crummy people if they'd been hanging out on Burnside late nights for very long.

I went inside the restaurant, went up to the counter and bought a large coffee. Once I got the drink I went and sat at a table near the front windows. I could see the two kids standing outside talking animatedly. Once they both turned and saw me in the window. I smiled and waved in what I hoped was a non-threatening manner. That seemed to spur a decision on the part of the young woman because she shrugged at her partner and headed towards the door. After a moment of hesitation the young guy looked my way once more. I could see he was terribly afraid, but to his credit he followed along behind the young woman. They both came through the door and walked over to my table. As they approached I pulled out my wallet and took out a twenty dollar bill and set it down in plain view. When they were close enough I said, "I'm glad you decided to come on in. Take this twenty and order what you want. I'll wait here."

The guy quickly reached out to grab the bill but the girl checked him by saying, "Joe, hold on just a second." She turned to me and said, blushing as she did so, "Can you give us a second to get cleaned up a bit? We must look a mess." I nodded and she looked at Joe and tilted her head towards the restrooms. The guy shrugged and nodded and they both headed back and were gone for several minutes. While they were gone I sipped the bad coffee and tried to convince myself I wasn't a complete fool for spending time on these two kids. My impression was the pair weren't hardened street people and I was willing to try and work with them.

I saw the guy come out of the men's room and lean against the wall to wait for his partner. She emerged shortly thereafter. The two of them came back to my table and the girl took off her jacket and draped it across the plastic chair across from me. She then reached out and picked up the twenty, smiled tentatively and said, "Thank you for this. I hope you don't expect much change back, it has been a while since Joe and I had much of a dinner."

I responded by saying, "Sure, I told you I'd spring for food and I meant that. Get whatever you want and don't worry about the change. Of course, I also promised you forty bucks. We can settle up with that after the two of you eat." As I spoke, I noticed the girl was very pretty with brown eyes, light brown hair, and a petite figure. I stood up and said, "Not to get all formal on you but, as I said my name is Matt, what are your names?" I stuck out my hand to the guy as I said this.

He gave a start of surprise but seemingly automatically stuck his own hand out to shake. I noticed he had a nice strong grip. "My name is Joe. This is my girl friend Christine." I disengaged his hand and stuck my hand out to Christine, who took it with a firm grip and a smile.

"Good to meet the two of you. Sorry to hold you up. Get on over to the counter and order up and I'll keep working on this mud that passes for coffee here." At this both of them smiled and did as instructed. I sat back down and knew that my impressions were correct. The two of them were not ill mannered delinquents but just two kids very much down on their luck. I decided I was looking forward to hearing their story so I sat back, took a sip of coffee, grimaced at the bitter taste and settled in to wait.

XVIII

Joe and Christine returned with two plastic trays loaded with an improbable amount of food. They sat down across from me and set to with gusto. I gave them time to take the edge off their hunger before leaning forward with my elbows on the table and saying, "I told you I am not a cop. That is true, but I am a private investigator. I'm working on a case for a woman whose son was killed and found under the Burnside Bridge early this past Monday morning. I'm looking for anyone who might have seen anything Sunday night or early Monday morning that could shed some light on the case. I'm specifically interested in whether the victim was shot there at the site or if he was shot somewhere else and brought there afterwards." I noticed I had their full attention even though they did not pause in their meal. I continued and said, "The victim was a friend of a close personal friend of mine, so I have more than a professional interest in solving this thing. I'd like to provide some closure not only from the legal side of things, but also for my friend's piece of mind." I don't know why I brought up my personal attachment to the case with the kids; maybe because I thought that if I established a personal connection to the crime, they'd be more likely to open up.

Whatever the reason, it seemed to work. The two of them looked at each other and exchanged a look before Christine responded, "Yeah, we were there that night. It had been a pretty quiet night and we had decided to try and get some sleep. We had settled in behind one of the big boulders in the Japanese-American Park at about three when we heard a car stop right near where I first saw you tonight. Joe and I peeked over the boulder in time to see a guy come around the front of the car, open the passenger side door and drag another guy out and pull him up onto the grass." Christine stopped there and Joe continued by saying, "Christine ducked down and pulled me down and we didn't look again until after we heard the car drive away. Once it was gone we looked again and saw the guy still laying there. We didn't go check out the person who'd been drug out of the car, but decided to get the heck out of there. We didn't know if the guy was dead or just passed out drunk or something else and didn't want to find out. We grabbed our stuff and took off down along the river to the other place we hang out by the Morrison Bridge."

I nodded and asked, "Can you tell me what kind of car it was? Also did you hear any shots?" Joe responded by saying, "Nope, definitely no shots. The car was a big black one but I couldn't tell what kind." Christine added, "I bet your next question is did we see plates. The answer is, no, we didn't get a chance to see a license plate. It was kind of freaky to see something like that and we did not want the driver to see us."

I grinned at Christine and said, "Sure, you're right about my next question. I understand about your not wanting to risk being seen. How about the person who got out of the drivers side? Did you get any details on what he looked like, are you sure it was a guy?"

The kids looked at each other and then turned back to me and Joe said, "No, not really but I'm pretty sure it was a guy because of the way he pulled the person out of the passenger's side. It didn't seem to be too difficult for him. You know how dark it is down there, but I think the guy had on dark clothes and I know he had some kind of baseball cap on. You gotta understand all this took place very fast and we didn't have a lot of time. Once the car drove away, I just wanted to get Christine out of there as soon as possible." At this he turned to her with a look of such obvious affection I couldn't help but start to like him.

"Okay," I said, "Can you think of anything else you saw or heard that might help me out? What you've said so far has been really helpful. It's clear that the shooting did not happen under the bridge. That might be really significant for the police." At this I noticed them both stiffen and I continued, "Its okay. I'm friends with the lead detective on this and he is a good guy. I've got to turn anything I learn over to him if it'll help solve the crime. I'm sure you understand that, right?" They both nodded somewhat reluctantly and I continued, "The detective might want to speak to you but I promise I'll be there with you. I will also try and just relay what you've told me and see how that goes. Either way you did nothing wrong and you don't have anything to worry about."

Christine said somewhat defiantly, "Okay, but we have our own reasons for not wanting to get involved with the cops." This seemed an opening for me so I followed up on her open ended declaration by asking, "Sure, I'm not particularly interested in any bad things you may have done before we met. I am, however, interested in your story. My gut tells me you are both pretty decent people and I don't understand why you are living on the street. I admit this is really none of my business and if you want to leave it at that I'd understand. That said I'm willing to help you out if you are in a jam." I sat back and waited as they exchanged another look.

Joe nodded at Christine and she returned the nod and turned to me and said, "Joe and I grew up in Edmonds, north of Seattle. We went to the same schools pretty much all our lives and began a relationship way beyond friendship in high school. Our parents just could not accept that we wanted to be together. They pretty much made our lives a living hell. It's all about the color of our skin with them, both sets of parents being equally against our being together. It makes no sense to Joe or me. We just couldn't take it any more. We stuck it out long enough to get through high school and finally took off and tried to make it on our own. For a while it was good and we had a little place and crappy jobs but we were together. Then the families found us and wouldn't let us be. It was getting really ugly and was probably going to get worse. We packed up what little we had, and that just barely filled two backpacks, and hitched our way down to Portland a month or so ago. It's been tough down here. We can't get jobs because we don't have a permanent address and the Oregon economy is terrible." At this juncture she paused and took a big breath and her eyes suddenly filled with tears and she clenched her fists on top of the table and I could see her will herself to hold it together. This was one strong kid. My opinion of Christine soared.

I let the silence hang, not wanting to push but knowing they needed to get some more stuff out. Joe filled the silence by stating, "Look, Matt, this last month has been hell but we're going to make it. What I can't stand is the thought of Christine getting hurt. We've gotten a little desperate the last couple of weeks and the fact that I can't keep her safe is killing me." That was enough to choke him up and he stopped. Christine put her arm around his shoulders and they turned, put their foreheads together, and seemed to draw strength from each other.

At that moment I made a snap decision that I hoped would not come back to bite me. I said, "It seems to me as if the two of you just need one good break to get you out of this tough spot you are in. This may sound crazy since I've just met you, especially the circumstances of our first meeting with you pulling a knife on me, Joe, and me threatening to pull a gun on you, but I'm willing to help. I'm not going to give or loan you money, mostly because I don't have much, but I can give you a safe place to stay until you get on your feet. I'll try and pull some strings and see about getting you jobs, nothing fabulous but I've got a couple of ideas, and get you started. After that it is up to you." I could see from the looks on their faces that they were completely taken aback by my offer. I continued by saying, "This is probably something the two of you need to talk about without me sitting here staring at you. What I could do is walk back down and get my truck, which I parked just off Burnside in China Town, and let you talk it through. I promise I'll be back. If you are not ready to make a call by then, that's fine. Just wave me on when I pull up outside the window here." I paused to pull out my bifold wallet from which I removed one of my business cards. "Here is my card in case you want to think about it and call me later. If you decide to give it a shot, just be waiting outside and I'll pick you up and we'll go get your stuff. Okay?" They both nodded numbly, seemingly still stunned by my proposal. I stood up, took two twenty dollar bills out of my wallet, and set them on the table. I then told them I'd be back in a short while and walked out the doors without waiting for a response.

I shook my head thinking of Holly's reaction to my presumptive new room mates. After a couple of blocks, I realized she would have done the same thing which put a smile on my face. Not caring what the night owls still walking the streets thought, I began whistling one of my favorite Disney tunes, *Beautiful Briny* from the movie Bedknobs and Broomsticks. My bubbly mood lasted for a block or so and then I became a little bit more somber as it dawned on me just how risky my decision to bring two strangers into my home was. I forcibly cleared my mind of the sudden doubts, knowing I'd cast those dice and wouldn't back out.

I was just about ready to make a left onto the street where I'd parked when I heard a car approaching from behind me. I don't know what made me half turn, maybe a change in engine pitch, but out of the corner of my eye I saw a dark sedan pulling along side me with the window down. What definitely caught my attention was the face in the driver's side window was masked. My instincts took over as I saw a flash of movement in the window and I threw myself on the sidewalk and behind a parked car. At that moment a couple of shots rang out and I heard the car accelerate and move away gaining speed. I had rolled up close against the parked car and automatically pulled my Colt but I took a moment to catch my breath as I'd landed awkwardly and dinged my shoulder on the way down. After listening for a moment I got to my knees and looked through the windows of the car in time to see a dark colored sedan disappear up and over Burnside Bridge.

As I whooshed a jittery deep breath and stood up, I realized my knees were knocking. Realizing the Colt was not going to do me any good, I went ahead and re-holstered it. I took a moment to check my surroundings and realized the street was devoid of any people. I didn't blame anyone who might have been hanging around for beating feet. I pulled out my cell phone and pulled up Ben Canfield's number, figuring he'd be awake at his hospital vigil. My guess was right because he answered right away. He said somewhat grumpily I thought, "Hey, Matt, are you suffering from insomnia? I told you I'd call if anything changed here."

I responded tersely by saying, "Well, Ben, I figured you'd want to know that I was just party to a drive by shooting here on Burnside right near the base of the bridge. Dark sedan. No I was not hit, and no, I did not get any plates or other details. Sorry to bother you, buddy."

Ben's tone was conciliatory as he answered, "Matt, good grief! I'm glad you are okay. Let me hang up and get some blues headed your way. Dave just came in to relieve me and I'll get down there as fast as I can." I told him that I'd stick tight and we hung up. I figured I'd better get a message to Joe and Christine so they wouldn't think I'd bailed out on them, so I called directory assistance and got the number of the burger place and placed the call. I told the female voice who answered the line that I'd just been in the restaurant and needed to get a message to my friends and asked if she could see if they were still there. After a short pause the voice came back on and said there was a young couple sitting by the front windows. I thanked her and told her that their names were Joe and Christine and asked if she could put one of them on the line. She agreed. After a moment Christine's voice came on the line.

I said, "Christine, I've just had a complication and will be a bit delayed in coming back. I'm just calling to make sure you don't think I bailed out on you because that is not the case at all. If you just sit tight there, I will swing back by, I promise. It just might be a while."

Christine responded by saying, "Joe and I have already decided to accept your incredibly kind offer, Matt. We'll sit here for as long as we need to." She paused and said with some concern in her voice, "Are you okay, Matt? Is there anything we can do?"

I said, "Sure, I am fine; not to worry. It'd be best if you just hold on there. Keep plugging away on all that food. You can't possibly have finished it off already." She laughed and said they'd do just that and we hung up.

XIX

I DID NOT HAVE to wait long before a police cruiser pulled up alongside the curb in front of me. The two uniformed officers both got out of the car and approached me. As they did so I called out, knowing policemen don't like to be surprised, "I'm Matt MacKinnon and I do have a firearm in a holster under my arm. I can show you my concealed weapons permit and PI license if you want."

One of the officers responded by saying, "Sure, Matt, I don't know if you remember me but I'm Tom Landingham. We met when you were working on a case a few months back."

I looked at the officer a bit more closely as he approached and did recognize him. We'd met briefly when I had been engaged in a case that had started out as a cheating wife investigation and turned into murder. I stuck out my hand; we shook, and I said, "You bet, Tom, I do remember meeting you. Good to see you again. I don't have a lot to say about this shooting. I'm working on that case involving the guy found dead under the bridge here last Monday on behalf of the mother. I came down to see if I could find any witnesses and was walking back to my truck when a dark sedan pulled alongside and started blasting away." Both officers had pulled out small notebooks from their shirt pockets and had begun jotting down notes as I spoke. I continued by saying, "When the car pulled alongside me and I saw a masked face in the driver's window I hit the deck as fast as I could. By the time I got back up the car was moving out fast across the bridge. There were two shots. Thankfully they both missed but they obviously smashed this store front glass up pretty good."

Tom nodded and the three of us turned to the storefront to look at the damage. At that moment Ben pulled up in an unmarked unit. He parked, got out of his car and walked up to us. We exchanged handshakes and he said, "Glad to see you in one piece, Matt. Did you tell the guys here your story?"

I answered by saying, "Yep, I pretty much laid out the basics, Ben; we had just started to look for the bullet holes as you showed up." I paused and we both turned to join the two uniforms. One of the plate glass windows of the small suite of offices had been totally shattered by the bullets. Ben asked one of the officers to work on getting the contact information of the office owner for notification purposes. Tom's partner did that and the three of us continued to search for the bullets. It wasn't long before Tom called out that he found a hole in the drywall on the far side of the office. We continued searching for a second bullet but were not successful in locating any further damage. At that point the other officer returned and said he had gotten a hold of the business owner who had been very grumpy indeed upon being informed of the damage to his office.

I caught Ben's eye and cocked my head towards the street in a signal that I wanted to speak to him. He nodded and we both stepped back out on the sidewalk. He said, "What's up, Matt?"

I brought him completely up to speed on my interaction with Christine and Joe and when I came to the part where I told the two of them I would help them out he shook his head and said, "Why is this not a surprise to me. I think you are nuts to do something like that but it is your house."

I shrugged and said, "I can understand why you would think that I'm crazy but I really do think these kids just need a break. What I want to ask is if you want to talk to them directly now or if you can just hold off and just go with what I've told you?"

He thought for a moment before saying, "I think I can go with what you've told me for now. Of course their story means this is clearly not just a case of Peterson being in the wrong spot at a bad time. The random mugging theory is completely out the window. You can imagine that I will probably have to interview them at some time, right?" I nodded and he continued, "Assuming they don't rob you blind and that they do stick around your place I can just go with that. You're probably done here for now. I'll let you know if we do dig a bullet out of that hole and what we learn if we do." I thanked him and as I turned to leave he said, "Good luck with those kids, Matt."

I called out a good bye to Tom and the other officer as I continued my rudely interrupted walk to my truck. I unlocked the door, got in, started it up and pulled away from the curb thinking how much had happened since I'd parked there a relatively short time ago. It did not take me very long to pull up in front of the restaurant where I'd left Joe and Christine. I could see them sitting at the same table as before and I honked once and waved when they looked my way. They both came out, I opened the passenger's side door, and the clambered in. Joe said, "Everything alright?" and I said, "Yep, I'll fill you in later. Shall we go get your stuff?"

Christine directed me down to the spot where they'd stashed their back packs and they quickly retrieved them and we turned back up Burnside and headed to my house. The ride home was quiet as I think we were all a bit uncertain on what we'd gotten ourselves into. I pulled into my driveway and asked them to follow me in. They grabbed their packs and did so without hesitation.

As we entered the living room I asked them if they wanted anything more to eat and they both politely declined. I could see they were beat so without further ado I led them into the bedroom I used as my guest room. I quickly got them settled in, gave them a quick tour of the second bathroom, and set them up with towels. I said, "Feel free to use the shower and make your selves comfortable. I'm beat and am ready to hit the hay. If you don't need anything else I'm going to do just that."

Christine said, "This is absolutely wonderful, Matt, we can't thank you enough for your kindness. It has been a long time since we slept anywhere near this comfortable and I feel like I'm in a dream."

I answered by saying, "Sure, you are welcome and no rush to get up in the morning. Good night." With that I turned down the hall and went into my bedroom. I remembered my promise to call Holly and debated briefly whether to hit the shower first or make the call. I decided to call figuring I'd just want to go to sleep after a hot shower. Holly answered her phone with a slightly groggy, "Hey, Matt, everything okay?"

I told her, "Everything is fine, Holly, no worries. I'll bring you up to speed sometime tomorrow, okay?" She said that would be fine and I knew she would be lights out very soon after she hung up. I picked up my Colt, cleared it, and put it in a drawer in my bedside table.

I stripped off my clothes, and headed to the bathroom. I took a very short but welcome shower and heard the water running in the other bathroom so knew Christine or Joe was doing the same thing. Once I was done I quickly dried off and slid under the covers. I tossed and turned for a very short time before it was lights out for me. My last conscious thought before falling asleep was I hoped my first impressions on Joe and Christine's character was correct or else I'd have a very rude awakening. I decided that was a problem for tomorrow and drifted off.

XX

I WOKE TO THE sound of a flock of black capped chickadees chirping outside my bedroom window and thought that was a good omen for the day. I looked at the clock and saw it was just past nine. I flung back the covers, jumped up, and hit the bathroom to take care of the usual morning ritual. That completed I headed out to the kitchen and got started on coffee and breakfast and, after thinking for a moment about dinner, opened my freezer and pulled out a venison roast which I placed in a bowl on the counter.

I was cutting up omelet fixings when I heard the guest room door open and Christine's voice call out, "good morning, Matt". I responded with a "good morning" of my own and turned just in time to see her disappear into the bathroom. After a short while she came out wearing what looked like the same shorts as she had on the night before and a wrinkled T-shirt and I asked, "Feel like some breakfast?"

She responded by saying, "That sounds great. Can I do anything to help?" I told her she could get started on toast and pointed to the bread drawer with my paring knife. We worked in companionable silence and I could sense her working up to saying something. She cleared her throat and said, "Matt, Joe and I talked before we fell asleep and we want you to know how much we appreciate you taking us in. We also know that our being here is a burden on you. We do not want to impose on you any more than we already have. We would understand completely if you asked us to leave at any time." She paused and reached into one of her pockets and pulled out two twenties, presumably the ones I'd given them last night, and said, "We want to return your forty dollars. It doesn't seem right to take your money given you are putting us up."

I said, "Well, Christine, I'm okay having you both around for a while so don't worry about that. Why don't we just take it day by day, okay? I told you I'd try and pull some strings to find you some work and I will get started on that today. Just relax and make yourself at home and recuperate at bit. If you need to do laundry the washer and dryer are out in the garage, help yourself. Besides that just make yourselves at home and relax. As far as the forty bucks go why don't you hang on to it? If you want to consider it a loan we can talk about that later."

She smiled a very relieved smile; put the twenties back in her pocket and said, "That sounds perfect, thanks." I asked her if she liked omelets and if yes what she liked in them and she said, "I love omelets and whatever you have would be fantastic."

I poured some scrambled egg mixture into a small frying pan and sprinkled in flaked smoked steelhead, chopped green onions, mushrooms, and shredded pepper jack cheese. After giving the eggs a minute or so to set I flipped the contents of the pan over in half and sprinkled some more cheese on top. Just then the toaster popped and I asked Christine to get the butter and jam out of the fridge. I pointed to the silverware drawer when she asked where the knives were. She busied herself buttering the toast and I pulled plates out of the cupboard. As we worked we exchanged idle chit chat. When the eggs were done I slid the omelet onto a plate, added a couple of pieces of toast, and suggested she sit down and set to without waiting. She did so without hesitation. I asked her if she drank coffee and she said, "no, but a glass of water would be great" and I complied.

I had just cracked another couple of eggs into the bowl when Joe emerged from the bedroom, called out, "good morning," and headed to the bathroom for his own morning ritual. I asked Christine if Joe was into omelets and she said, "I know he would love one just like this, Matt, it is excellent." I replicated what I'd done for Christine's omelet and finished just as Joe came out of the bathroom. I said, "Hey, Joe, you're just in time to pull up a seat. Christine said you'd probably eat an omelet if I made you one."

He quickly sat down and said, "Wow, this looks great. Thank you." I asked if he wanted some coffee or anything else to drink and he said, "Water would be great." I set him up and went to work on my own omelet. When it was done I took my plate and sat down across from them.

After a good start on my breakfast I said, "Joe, Christine and I already had a talk but I want you to know that you are both welcome to hang out here. We agreed to just take things day by day. Don't worry about anything for now. I'm going to make a couple of calls and see if I can get you some work. I need to take off but feel free to hang around here if you like. I'm not sure when I'll be back but my guess would be around dinner time. I'll probably invite my girl friend Holly over and I'm sure she'd like to meet the two of you. The four of us could have dinner if you are up for that."

The two of them nodded and Christine said, "That sounds great." We finished eating and I stood up and took my dishes to the sink. Christine said, "Please let us clean up Matt."

I said, "You talked me into it, Christine, thanks." I set my dishes down and headed to my bedroom where I got dressed in jeans and orange Oregon State polo. After a moments debate, I pulled the Colt out of the bedside table drawer and donned the holster. When I was finished I went back out into the kitchen and saw Joe and Christine had gotten started on cleaning up. They both noticed the gun under my arm and looked a bit startled but did not say anything. I told them I was headed out, they called out "good byes", and I walked downstairs to the front door. I pulled on a light wind breaker before going out the door.

Once I was sitting in my truck I pulled out my cell phone and dialed Andrea Loughton's number. Andrea was a woman I had met when I was working the cheating wife turned murder case a few months back. At one point during that investigation I'd considered her a prime murder suspect but had been proven very wrong. We'd met for lunch several times since then and gotten to know each other quite well. She was a senior executive at a big electronics firm. I considered her a good friend and was comfortable running my request by her.

I heard her familiar voice say, "Hey, Matt, good to see your name pop up on my caller ID. How are you doing?"

I responded by saying, "I'm doing well, Andrea, thanks. I have a pretty big favor to ask. How about I spring for lunch and fill you in?" Sounding intrigued she said that would be fine and we agreed to meet at one of our favorite spots, Kells Irish Pub, at 12:30. We hung up and I sat for some moments thinking. I hoped Andrea might be able to pull some strings and fix Joe up with a job on a loading dock of one of the warehouses her firm operated. My idea for a job for Christine was much closer to home. I decided to just walk up to check out that lead. The Vista Spring Café is a very nice place only a couple of blocks from my house. I'd spent a lot of time there over the years and knew the owner very well. I knew the place wouldn't be open yet but people would be there getting ready for the lunch-time traffic.

It took me about three minutes to walk to the café (a fact I relished on those nights I went out for drinks there) and I went around to the back door and knocked. I was happy to see Joyce, the owner, open the door. After exchanging hellos I said, "Joyce, I remember that you were hiring wait staff a few days ago when I came for lunch. Did you fill that job yet?"

She said, "Nope, not yet, Matt. Do you have someone in mind?" I told her I did but I should probably give her a short history so she asked me to come in. She poured a couple of cups of her very good coffee and gestured for me to follow her into the back office. I did so and we sat. I laid out my story about meeting Joe and Christine. I concluded by saying, "You can probably understand why I wanted to give you this low down, Joyce. I think I've got a pretty good read on Christine's character but I did not want to spring anything on you."

She nodded speculatively and said, "Yes, I appreciate your candor, Matt. I guess I'm willing to take a chance on this young woman if you are. Why don't you have her come in later today after the lunch time rush is over and I'll have a talk with her? If I get the same impressions as you have I'd be happy to give her a shot."

"Thanks very much for your consideration Joyce. I'll give Christine the message and I'm sure she'll be here." We stood up, shook hands, and I walked back out onto the street and headed for my house. I went inside and saw that my house guests were just finishing drying and putting away the breakfast dishes. I said, "Christine, I just set up an appointment for you to interview with my friend Joyce who owns the Vista Spring Café. I remembered she was looking for wait staff and assumed that you would be willing to give that a shot. Sound okay?"

Christine said, "Gee, Matt, you don't waste any time do you? I'd love to speak to Joyce and thanks for setting that up!"

I said, "Not a problem. I'm working on something for you as well, Joe, and have a lunch date with someone to talk about that. I'll keep you posted. Please do feel free to answer my phone if it rings, okay? I don't get many calls on my home phone so if it does ring it is liable to be me." The two of them agreed. I gave them a rundown on the workings of the TV and sound system and then said "see you later" and left. Feeling the need to burn off some energy I started up my truck and headed down the hill towards my club content that I had done what I could to fulfill my promise to Christine and Joe.

XXI

I WAS HAPPY TO see Monique back behind the front desk of the club. We called out cheerful hellos and she said, "How's the day going, Matt?" I assured her it was better now and would only be more so after I had a good swim.

One of the best things about swimming is that once I got in a groove I could let my mind wander. As I made my first turn I thought about where I was, or wasn't, on the case I was working on. I felt pretty good about meeting up with Joe and Christine and discovering that the killing had almost certainly taken place somewhere besides under the bridge where the body was dumped. I was not at all as satisfied with my lack of progress with the Petersons, particularly the Mr., and I was sure there was something going on that was somehow tied to Doug's death. The fact that Peterson senior had suddenly done an about face and started giving his son cash above and beyond the trust fund he and his wife had bickered so much over did not make sense. Based on what little I had gleaned during my brief interview it struck me that Peterson did not have the personality to back down and suddenly decide to be more giving for what he considered a wastrel son.

It may be my mind has become jaded because of my line of work, I have had dealings with many shady characters, but I couldn't help but consider blackmail as a reason for such a change of heart. And of course blackmail had led to murder countless times over the course of human history.

I needed to run my ideas by someone else. Ben seemed like an immediate first choice and I decided to call him immediately after my lunch date with Andrea. That decision made I poured on the coals and proceeded to finish my swim with a flourish. I looked up at the clock on the wall when I touched the side after completing a mile and saw I had plenty of time to get to Kells in time for my meeting with Andrea.

XXII

I WAS LUCKY ENOUGH to find a parking spot less than two blocks away from Kells on 2nd Avenue. After adding money to the meter and the short walk I was right on schedule and walked through the door just in time to get the last table for two on restaurant side of the establishment. I told the waitress that I was waiting for a friend. As I said that the door opened and one of the most beautiful women I've ever known walked through the door and straight towards me. Andrea Loughton had a classic blonde, blue eyed beauty that was backed up by a direct and humorous personality I very much enjoyed. She at first came across as a very cool, aloof person but as I'd gotten to know her I had learned that aspect of her character was a sort of defense mechanism to protect herself in the sexist, male dominated business at which she excelled.

I stood, we exchanged a warm embrace, and we settled into our seats and busied ourselves with menus for a moment. I looked up as I set my menu down and noticed that Andrea was looking at me with a quizzical expression on her face. I looked a question at her and she said, "Must be a pretty big favor if you're willing to spring for lunch here, Matt. Why don't you just get that off your chest so we can enjoy our lunch?"

"Sure," I responded, "You aren't one to beat around the bush are you, Andrea?" I proceeded to lay out pretty much the same story as I had for Joyce at the Vista Spring Cafe and concluded by saying, "I think I've got Christine all lined up but am still working on a possible job for, Joe. That's where you come in. I know he is a high school graduate but he can't have a lot of job related skills given what he told me he's been doing since they graduated. I figured he might work out as a laborer on one of your loading docks. If you think I'm out of line I know you will tell me."

She chuckled and said, "Boy is that all you're after? If so, that is not a big deal at all and I'm perfectly willing to help. Excuse me for a moment." With that she pulled her cell phone out of her purse, dialed a number, smiled a glorious smile at me and when a muted voice answered said, "Larry, Andrea Loughton here. Have you got a moment?" Pause while the voice answered, "I've got a kid who needs some work and might be good in your shop. You need any help?" Another pause and she continued, "Yeah that sounds good and thanks. Should I just have the kid report to your office directly?" The voice mumbled a few more words and Andrea said, "Okay, I'll pass that along. I won't forget you at Christmas time, Larry. Talk to you later." With that she hung up her phone and turned her attention back to me. "Have you got a pen and paper, Matt?" I nodded, took out my notebook and a pen, and looked at her expectantly. Andrea said, "Have Joe show up at our warehouse on North River Street and check in at the office tomorrow at eight sharp. He should ask for a guy named Larry Rutter. Larry will set him up and put him to work." She paused while I wrote down the address and then continued in a very businesslike tone, "You might want to make it clear to Joe that if he works hard it'll be great. If he doesn't he'll be out on his ear in short order. Larry is a no nonsense kind of guy which is why he and I get along. You heard me tell him I won't forget him at Christmas time and what that means for you is a bottle of Chivas Regal because I know that is his drink of choice. Okay?"

"Sure," I responded, "That seems perfectly reasonable to me and I will make that clear to Joe. The favor part of this deal is over and the rest is totally up to him. Thanks for this Andrea. Now, how about that lunch I promised?" Andrea agreed and I nodded at the waitress who had been looking our way expectantly and who when I nodded came over promptly. Andrea ordered the corned beef and cabbage with a Black and Tan. I said, "Make that two exactly the same." You can never go wrong ordering corned beef and cabbage at Kells. The food is always excellent and the Black and Tans a perfect drink to accompany the food.

Andrea and I had not seen each other for a couple of weeks so we spent the rest of the time together catching up and exchanging light hearted banter. We finished our lunches, I paid the check adding a generous tip, and we stepped out onto the sidewalk. We turned towards each other; Andrea took my hands in hers, leaned in and gave me a quick peck on the cheek. She leaned back and said, "Nice to see you Matt. Take care of yourself."

I swallowed hard, the woman always had that affect on me, but only said, "You bet, Andrea, thanks again for the favor. Have a nice rest of the week." With that we both turned and walked our separate ways. As was always the case I found myself turning around for one last wave. I wasn't disappointed as Andrea had also turned around. We laughed out loud and exchanged mock salutes knowing that we both felt the powerful attraction between us.

XXIII

As I slowly walked towards my truck I pulled my phone out of my pocket and dialed my home number. After a couple of rings Christine picked up and said, "Matt MacKinnon's residence, this is Christine speaking." I said, "Hi, Christine, Matt here. Is Joe still there?" She responded affirmatively and called out and Joe came on the line. "Hey, Matt, what's up?"

I filled him in on the part of my lunch conversation that affected him and he thanked me profusely when I told him the news. I said, "Sure, no problem but I have to tell you Andrea was quite serious when she said the favor part is over and you are going to have to work up to Larry's standards or else." Joe assured me that he wouldn't let me down and I told him I'd see him later. Just before we broke the connection I heard him whoop with joy. I smiled at his enthusiasm and knew he'd work out just fine.

That bit of business taken care of I decided to follow through on my decision to run my blackmail idea by Ben Canfield. He answered his phone promptly and said, "If you are looking for a payback for picking up yesterday's lunch tab you are too late, I just finished a lousy lunch here at my desk."

I chuckled and responded by saying, "Nope, I'm going to hold you to that but I just finished off a big plate of Kells corned beef and cabbage. Not to rub it in but it was fabulous as usual. What I'm calling about is the Peterson case. I've got some ideas I want to run by you if you have any time."

"Well, normally I'd be all ears, Matt, but I am seriously swamped here. Can you give me the cliff notes for now just to prime my pump?" Ben said.

I responded by saying, "Blackmail. I thought about this whole deal of the father having a change of heart and bumping up the amount he gave to Doug and it does not wash. One plausible explanation is Doug had something on his father and was using it for leverage. The older Peterson caved for a time but ended up taking drastic action to put a stop to it."

There was a long pause on Ben's part and I had just taken a breath to ask if he was still there when he spoke, "Yep, I can see that but I sure as heck can't pull anything concrete out of what we have to work with from a legal standpoint. You know it would be impossible to get a warrant based on what we have. Any ideas on what you're going to do from here?"

After a short pause of my own I said, "Well, keeping some pressure on the parents seems like it could produce some results if I am correct. Lacking any other brilliant idea that's probably what I'll do." Changing the subject on him I said, "Hey, if you are at your desk that must mean there's been a change in Gillian's condition. What's up there?"

He cleared his throat and said, "Oh hell, I am sorry I forgot to call. Yes, she came around earlier this morning and the docs think she'll be just fine in time. Lots of physical therapy on her shoulder but she seems determined. We had another crisis downtown that I got called away on or I would have called you as I promised. Dave and I took her statement. She didn't have a lot to say. After she left you she said she stuck her head into the meeting where Eleanor was and learned she was settled in for the duration of that zoo meeting. Gillian decided to go get her briefcase and do some work in the lobby while waiting for the meeting to get over. She had almost reached the car when she heard a shot. Her last impression before passing out was that she'd been kicked by a mule. She remembers nothing else until she woke up in her hospital bed. We spoke to the parking attendant. She heard the shot and ran to see what was going on. She's the one who found Gillian and called 911. If she hadn't acted so quickly Gillian might not have made it. The parking attendant did not see any cars exit the garage, and if any had they would have had to gone past her, so it is certain the shot came from some one on foot. There are several ways out for foot traffic so no help there. Security cameras are haphazardly scattered throughout the structure, and we pulled the tapes and have someone reviewing them, but coverage isn't that great. Not a lot of hope there. Hey, Matt, my Captain is beckoning so I gotta go. I'll call you later." With that he hung up.

I stopped and leaned my back against the brick wall of a building down the street from Kells. I was debating my options and I quickly reached the conclusion that I would get nowhere with Earl Peterson. I doubted he'd even agree to see me. That left me with trying to get another interview with Eleanor. Even though I was working for her I had no doubt I was in her doghouse after having the gall to interrupt her social event.

I dialed her number and found myself wondering if she'd already replaced Gillian. Much to my surprise I recognized her voice when the connection was made. I said in a business like manner, "Ms. Peterson, this is Matt MacKinnon. We need to talk. Do you have time if I came over soon?"

I was not surprised by the icy tone of her voice when she responded, "Well, Mr. MacKinnon, despite what you might think I do not just sit around my home waiting for people like you to call." I grimaced to myself at the tone of her voice when she said people like you and knew I had an uphill battle.

I was determined not to be cowed by her and butted in before she could continue by saying, "Ms. Peterson, your son has been murdered, your personal assistant's life is hanging by a thread (I gambled that she hadn't taken the time to check on Gillian so I deliberately stretched the truth), and I narrowly avoided being either dead or in a hospital myself from a third shooting." As I said this I heard her gasp so I knew the last was news to her but I continued, "The case you hired me to investigate has blown up and I need some answers."

"Alright," she said sounding as if she were going to choke, "Please be here in about an hour. I will have to re-arrange a meeting I had scheduled." At that I heard a click and knew she had hung up to try and demonstrate she was still in charge of our relationship.

XXIV

I DECIDED I HAD time to drop by Providence hospital for a quick visit with Gillian so jumped in my truck and pulled into traffic. As I entered the hospital parking garage I took a few moments to scope out the area before walking over to the exit. I was happy not to see any lurking strangers pointing guns at me. I entered the front doors and stepped up to the reception area and asked the attendant if she could direct me to Gillian Anderson's room. I was even happier that she did so with brisk efficiency and a smile. I headed down the hall following her instructions. Before getting on the elevator to the upper floor I stopped at the gift store that was on the way to the room and picked up a small floral arrangement.

The front desk attendant's instructions were right on and I had no trouble locating the room I was looking for. I stopped in front of the partially closed door to the room I had been directed to and knocked softly. A distinguished looking older man opened the door and looked at me inquiringly. I said, "Excuse me, my name is Matt MacKinnon and I am looking for Gillian Anderson."

The man nodded and said, "Hello, Mr. MacKinnon, my name is Robert Anderson. I am Gillian's father. Thank you for coming." We exchanged handshakes and he stepped back opening the door so I could enter.

Gillian was lying in a bed that was tilted up so she was half way sitting up. She looked much better than I thought a person who had just had a bullet removed from their shoulder would. A pleasant looking older woman sitting in a chair by the bedside stood as I approached.

She introduced herself as Elizabeth Anderson, Gillian's mother, and I shook her hand and said, "Nice to meet you, Mrs. Anderson. I am Matt MacKinnon."

I turned my attention to Gillian and said, "Gillian, I am very sorry that you were hurt so badly. I can't help but feel that you were shot because you met with me. I'm sorry for that and am very relieved to see you looking so well." I smiled at her and said, "I'd much rather we were meeting in the bar in Kincaid's instead of here. How about we make that date and you let me know when you are ready?"

Gillian smiled back at me and I heard dutiful chuckles from her mother and father at my attempt at humor. She responded by saying, "That sounds like a very good offer to me, Matt, and if the doctors are correct I'll be out of here very soon. I actually feel pretty good but I'm sure that is due to the magic that comes out of the pharmacy."

I belatedly remembered the flower arrangement I held in my left hand but held it out to Gillian's mother and said, "It's not much but I am in between appointments and hoped this would brighten up the room a bit." I looked around the room and noticed for the first time there were rather a lot of flowers. I said, "Looks like I'm not the only one who hoped to cheer you up with flowers."

Gillian laid back, smiled and said, "My friends have been wonderful as have my parents." At that she looked at her mother and father with obvious affection. Her face turned serious as she continued by saying, "Are your appointments related to Doug's murder? If they are I hope you are being extremely careful. I do not want you to wind up in the bed next door!"

Thinking it not a great idea to bring her fully up to speed on what had transpired since she had wound up in the hospital I just said, "Yep, I'm still plugging away. Some progress but overall it is pretty slow going. Speaking of going I hate to bring flowers and run but I do need to head out. I'll stop by and check on you as soon as I can. I'm glad to meet you Mr. and Mrs. Anderson." They both responded in kind and we shook hands all around again.

As I headed out the door I heard Gillian call out, "Be very careful, Matt, Earl Peterson is a ruthless man."

XXV

As I pulled onto highway 26 away from the hospital towards downtown my mood went from optimism at Gillian's better than expected condition to morose as I contemplated my pending interview with Eleanor Peterson. To say I expected a negative reception would be putting it mildly. Of course my mission was to deliberately provoke some reaction so I figured I deserved whatever I got. My mind ranged over the possible reactions Ms. Peterson might have when I told her that her husband had been giving their son additional funds above and beyond the trust. If I were asked to bet I'd wager heavily that this would come as a surprise to her.

I pulled into the Peterson driveway once again and as I parked, got out of my truck and approached the front door, I resolved to stick with the respectful employee pose until I deemed that wasn't going to get me anywhere. I stopped on the front porch and rang the doorbell. After a very short wait the door opened and Ms. Peterson stood before me. She said rather curtly, "Thank you for being prompt Mr. MacKinnon. Please come in." With that she turned and walked down the hall. I followed her into the same office we had conducted our previous interviews.

This time Mrs. Peterson did not choose the convivial sitting around the coffee table routine as we had during my previous visits. She sat behind her ornate desk and said, "Please do have a seat, Mr. MacKinnon." She gestured at one of the two chairs set opposite her.

The respectful employee pose didn't last long enough for me to follow her instructions. As I sat down I asked, "Mrs. Peterson, how long have you known about the additional funds, besides those from the trust, your husband had been providing Doug?" She gaped at me clearly caught off guard by the aggressive tone of my inquiry. I continued, hoping to keep her back on her heels, "Your husband was very unhappy that you had engaged my services and expressed his displeasure during our interview. To be quite frank we had a very unpleasant conversation. It would have been nice if he had been kept in the loop on the terms of my assignment. I assumed you would inform him of your decision to hire me and I counted on having full cooperation from you and him." I could see her struggling to retain her composure so I decided to let up and not push my luck.

Her voice was shaking with what I took to be rage as she said, "You are way out of line Mr. MacKinnon. How dare you speak to me in that tone in my own home! I know nothing of my husband giving our son money outside the trust and am sure you are lying. My husband would never do that." I could see her fingers were clenched so tightly into her palms that her knuckles were white from the tension.

"Mrs. Peterson, I have it on very good authority that what I am saying is true." I knew that she would assume that the good authority was her husband from the context of my comments. I continued, "I can only assume that Doug had gotten himself into some sort of financial difficulty. If that is true such difficulty could easily be linked to his murder. Surely you can see that if he had become embroiled with unscrupulous business partners he could have been in danger?"

Her face drained of color and she choked out, "Unscrupulous business partners? You have no idea what you are talking about." She clasped her hands together and sat up and said, "I must ask you to leave this instant. You may consider yourself dismissed from my employ."

At that I stood, placed my hands flat on the top of the desk, and said, "Certainly, but if you think I am going to drop my inquiries just because you fired me nothing could be further from the truth. I will send you a final bill. Good day ma'am." I turned abruptly and walked to the front door and out into the cool clean air.

XXVI

I found I had to collect my thoughts as I prepared to drive away from the Peterson home for what I hoped was the last time. Mrs. Peterson was not the only one who had gotten worked up during our brief interaction. I was surprised by the fact I was so angry and had to think for a moment before I understood just what I was angry about. It dawned on me that I was utterly flabbergasted by the complete lack of sorrow I'd seen from both the Peterson's regarding the death of their son. Such cold hearted disregard for their only child was something I could not fathom.

Setting aside those thoughts with difficulty I started up my truck and headed down the driveway. I looked at the clock on the dashboard and saw that it was just past 3:30. I stopped at the end of the driveway and pulled out my phone and dialed Holly's number. I wanted to invite her for dinner and give her a heads up that we would have some unexpected company. She picked up and in her typical cheerful manner said, "Hey, Matt, how's the day going?"

I cleared my throat and said, "Well, it has been interesting since you and Alex left last night to say the least." I proceeded to succinctly bring her up to date on what had happened and concluded by saying, "So, I've got temporary roomies. Are you up for joining us for dinner and getting acquainted with them?"

I could hear amusement in her tone as she responded, "One thing I've learned is that you are rarely boring, Matt, but this time you've outdone yourself. I'd love to come over and meet Christine and Joe. Okay if I show up about 6:30 or so?"

"Yep, sounds good," I answered. With that Holly stated she was off to a meeting with the design team she was working with on a new product line. I closed my phone and debated whether I should call Ben Canfield but decided against it. With no other plans I decided it was time to head home. It took very little time to reach my house. As I pulled into the driveway I noticed the sidewalk in front of the house and walkway to the front stoop had been washed free of winter leaves and grit. I also saw Joe standing on a ladder with a squeegee and spray bottle of Windex washing windows. As he heard me pull in and close my door he turned and called out from his lofty perch, "Hi, Matt, hope you don't mind we decided to keep busy while you were gone?" With that he gave a final swipe on the window he was working on and clambered down the ladder.

I stopped and said, "I don't mind at all and thanks for your efforts. I haven't washed the outsides of my windows in well over a year. They look great."

I helped him pack up the ladder, bucket, and other supplies he'd been using and we put it all in the garage. That done we headed in through the backdoor. I could hear the latest Lady GaGa tune playing on the stereo with the vacuum running in the back room. As we took off our shoes I said to Joe, "Sounds like you were not the only one who has been busy."

Joe grinned at me and said, "I think Christine had pent up house chores energy. Pretty tough to get serious about cleaning up the rocks in the greenway where we had been hanging the last couple of weeks. I tried to help her inside but she booted me out of the house and told me to get busy outside. I haven't seen Christine this happy in a long time."

With that we headed through the kitchen into the living room. Turning down the tunes I hollered out, "Hey, Christine, I'm home." At that the vacuum turned off and Christine came down the hallway with a happy look on her face. She pushed a stray wisp of her light brown hair behind her ear and said, "Hi, Matt, sorry for the loud music. Hope that's okay?"

I told her, "Sure, cleaning house is unbearable without music. Not a problem." I noticed the kitchen and living room were spotless. I continued, "I'm impressed. I'd have taken in room mates a long time ago if I figured they were all as helpful as the two of you. I came home so I could get dinner started. My friend Holly is coming over about 6:30 and is looking forward to meeting you. How'd your interview with Joyce go?"

"Oh, Matt, it was awesome and Joyce hired me on the spot. I start tomorrow for the lunch shift. I can't begin to tell you how much I appreciate you talking to her."

Christine's heartfelt thanks left me feeling quite pleased with myself. Any lingering doubts I may have had relative to my snap decision to allow Joe and Christine into my home had evaporated. I looked at them both and said, "Well, it has been a pretty good day for both of you and I'm happy I could help you out. I need to get busy on dinner. When Holly gets here she is going to be famished. She is looking forward to meeting you both." I turned to the stereo and picked up the iPad that I had hooked into my receiver. "I do like Lady GaGa but how about a change of pace? You two up for some Blackfoot?" The two of them looked at me with blank expressions and I said, "Oh boy, you two are in for a real treat." I tapped a few times on the handy dandy iPad and the first chords of *Train, Train* led to smiles on both their faces. Christine returned to her vacuuming and Joe followed me into the kitchen. "I've never done any cooking. You mind if I watch?"

"Sure, but better yet you can help if you like." I answered. When he nodded I directed him to the drawer where I kept the potatoes. "Go ahead and scrub four of those up, give them a few pokes, and wrap them up in foil. We are going to do twice baked potatoes."

Joe nodded and went to work. I took the venison roast out of the fridge, unwrapped it, rinsed it off, and plopped it in a glass baking dish. Joe asked, "What is that?" and I told him it was a hind quarter roast from a Columbia black tail deer I'd taken with my bow the fall before. He looked impressed and our conversation turned to hunting. Joe had never done any hunting but was intensely interested. I had done a lot of hunting and enjoyed sharing my stories as most hunters do. As he worked on the spuds he watched me garnish the roast with fresh garlic cloves, black pepper, and Worcestershire sauce. I set the roast aside, turned the oven on to 350, and tossed in the cleaned and wrapped potatoes.

I asked Joe if he had gotten any lunch and he shook his head and said, "Nope, Christine was on fire and insisted we get the house cleaned up."

I said, "Well then, you must be starving. How about we whip up an appetizer?" He nodded eagerly and I opened the fridge, scanned the contents and after a moments thought pulled out prosciutto, cream cheese, purple onions, and Tiger sauce. I asked him to chop up the onion and prosciutto into very small pieces. While he was doing that I mixed dollops of Tiger Sauce into the cream cheese. He asked what we were making and I told him, "I have no idea but with these ingredients it can't be bad. We'll spread it on garlic bagel crisps I have left over from last night."

Once he was done I mixed everything together, sampled a small amount of the mixture, found it lacked a little zip so added a few more splashes of the Tiger Sauce. Once I was content I got the bagel crisps out of the cupboard and dumped them into a serving bowl. Just as I was about ready to call to Christine I heard the vacuum turn off and she came down the hallway.

I announced, "Time to call it a day. You both have done great and deserve a break. Let's take a load off and get a head start on Holly." I grabbed the bowls of spread and bagel crisps, walked into the living room, and set them down on the coffee table. I told Joe and Christine not to wait but go ahead and get started and headed back into the kitchen. I called out, "What do you want to drink, I'm having beer which of course is off limits for you but I've got lemonade, iced tea, and orange juice." They both opted for lemonade which I poured into two glasses with ice. I snagged a Fosters, twisted off the cap, and returned to the living room. I sat down in the recliner opposite the couch well within reach of the snacks.

My mouth was full of the savory spread Joe and I had put together when the phone on the side table next to my chair rang. I noticed Holly's name on the caller ID and swallowed just in time to say, "Hey, Holly, what's up?"

Her voice was as grim as I'd ever heard her sound when she said, "Matt, Alex and I came home to get our racquetball gear. She found her place had been completely trashed. We are at her place now and she is pretty upset."

I asked if they had called the police and she said, "No, not yet but that is next. Can you get down here?"

I said, "Sure, I'll also give Ben a call. Be there in a few." With that I hung up and told the kids, "That was Holly. There's been a bit of trouble at her friend's house and I'm headed over there." I gave them instructions on when to put in the roast before leaving and told them I'd check in if I was going to be late.

Before starting my truck I pulled out my phone and dialed Ben Canfield's number. He answered after a couple of rings with a tired sounding, "Hello, Matt." I said, "Holly just called and told me Alex's house has been ransacked. She is probably talking to someone in your building now. I'm just heading down there but thought I'd let you know. I have no idea if this is related to the Peterson homicide but it sure could be which is why I called you."

Ben said, "Sure, Matt, I'm ten minutes from Ms. Galloway's place so will meet you there." With that we hung up and I started up my truck and backed out the driveway. As I headed down SW Vista Ave I wondered why I had jumped to the conclusion that the events at Alex's house were tied to the case I was working on. At first blush it seemed like a stretch. I concluded that I did not have enough information to decide one way or another. What I did know was that Holly and Alex would be comforted by my presence and that was good enough for me.

XXVII

I had just parked in the lot at Holly and Alex's condo complex down by the river and gotten out of my truck when Ben pulled into a spot nearby. I waited for him to get out of his sedan and we shook hands and exchanged hellos before heading across the lot and up the walkway. I noticed a police cruiser parked in the lot and knew that one of the ladies had put a call in to police dispatch. Holly opened the door to Alex's place, which was on the ground floor, before I had the chance to ring the bell. She and I exchanged a hug and brief kiss hello. The three of us stepped inside and I saw Alex break off a conversation with two uniformed officers. She looked more angry than upset but her expression changed to a smile as I walked over and gave her a quick hug. I said, "Hi, Alex, pretty tough way to end a day uh?"

She responded by saying, "Yep, not exactly my idea of winding down after work for sure. Thanks for coming down, Matt." With that she turned to Ben, extended her hand and said, "Thank you for coming also Detective Canfield."

Ben shook Alex's hand and said, "You bet, Ms. Galloway, sorry we have to meet under these circumstances." He turned to one of the uniformed officers and asked, "What have you got Sarge?"

"Well, Detective, we just arrived shortly before you got here and had just started taking down Ms. Galloway's statement." He turned to Alex and said, "Ms. Galloway, you mentioned there was no sign of forced entry. Have you checked all the windows as well as the front and back doors?"

Alex nodded and said, "Yes, Holly and I checked all the windows.

They are closed, don't look like they were forced open and none of them are broken. Feel free to take a look around if you like."

The Sergeant said, "Sure, I doubt we'll see anything you did not but it can't hurt to double check." He turned to his partner and said, "Why don't you take a look around outside, Art?" The partner nodded and headed out the front door. Ben, the Sergeant, and I followed Alex down the short hallway past the one bathroom. I noticed Holly stayed behind and was busying herself in the kitchen.

It did not take very long to complete a circuit of Alex's condo. It was immediately clear that Holly's initial description of it being trashed was accurate. The two bedrooms, the bathroom, the living room, and kitchen had been thoroughly ransacked. Books pulled off the couple of book cases, all the drawers taken out and dumped, and closets rummaged. All of the windows and the sliding glass door that opened from the dining room to a small patio were intact.

The Sergeant asked Alex if anything had been stolen. Alex responded by saying, "It is hard to tell with all the mess but I did a little checking. I haven't been able to find a couple of fairly nice gold chains I had in a jewelry box on my dresser. I didn't have a lot of really nice jewelry to begin with. I can say that all of my stereo and computer stuff is still here. Besides the necklaces I think it will take some time to figure out if anything else is missing."

Once the tour was over the four of us went back to the dining room. Holly asked if anyone wanted coffee. The Sergeant politely declined, turned to Ben and said, "I think Art and I are done here Detective. I'll file my report back at the precinct and check in with you later." He turned to Alex and said, "We will be in touch if anything comes up Ms. Galloway. Here is my card, feel free to give me a call at any time." With that he tipped his hat, nodded goodbye to the rest of us, and Alex saw him out the door.

As Alex shut the door and turned back to the rest of us I said, "I'd take some coffee and thanks Holly." As she poured Holly looked at Ben and said as a question, "Ben?", and Ben nodded affirmatively. Holly poured a third cup and carried two of them to the dining room table where she set them down. Ben and I seated ourselves as Holly went to the kitchen and returned with a cup of her own and she sat down across from us. The three of us took sips as Alex poured a cup and joined us.

We sat in silence for a short time drinking our coffee before I said,

"Alex, I don't know what you think but it seems to me that this incident could be related to Doug's murder. If it is do you have any idea what someone might have been looking for?"

Alex paused a moment before responding, "The same thought occurred to me, Matt. I can say for sure that Doug did not give me anything to keep here during the time we dated. Of course I don't know if he hid something without my knowing but it seems unlikely. You can see how small my place is. There just aren't that many secure hiding places."

I nodded and Holly said, "I've been trying to figure out how someone could get in here during broad day light without attracting attention. The obvious answer seems to be whoever it was just looked like they belonged here. Are you missing any keys, Alex?"

Alex stood up and walked over to a small table near the front door and picked up a set of keys. She said, "Well, my key to the front and back door are here on my key chain." She set down the keys and walked over to a kitchen cupboard which she opened. I could see a set of hooks on the inside of the cupboard door with various keys hanging. Alex took a moment to look and said, "My backup keys are also all here." She shut the door and returned to the table.

I said, "I don't mean to be too personal here but did you give a key to your place to Doug by any chance?"

Alex glanced at Ben, seemed to color slightly and said, "Yes, I did, Matt. I am not sure what happens to personal effects and I hadn't thought about asking about my key. How does that work Detective?"

Ben set down his cup and somewhat ponderously said, "Well, Mr. Peterson's personal effects are all retained as evidence until the file is closed. I, of course, went through what was found on his person and at the scene where he was found but don't remember seeing any keys. Excuse me a moment, I think it is worth double checking that and I'll make a call to the precinct." With that he took out his phone, dialed a number and spoke briefly to the person on the other end. He hung up and said, "The guy I just spoke to will pull the evidence box and check for any keys and call me back."

I said, "My bet is your memory is just fine, Ben, and the answer will be there are no keys to be found. I'd also bet we've figured out just how someone got into your place, Alex. I'd highly recommend you change the locks on your doors ASAP."

Ben nodded and chimed in, "I agree with Matt entirely Ms. Galloway. Let me give you a number of a locksmith I've recommended many times. He is fair and works very quickly. I bet he'd come down here right now if you give him a call."

Alex said, "Sure that seems like a very good idea." She stood and walked over to the phone, picked it up and looked at Ben expectantly. Ben responded by giving her a number he had memorized. Alex dialed and was quickly connected to someone she conveyed her situation to. She then provided her address, thanked the person on the other end of the line and hung up. "The locksmith agreed to come right down. Thank you for the recommendation Detective. By the way would you mind just calling me Alex? Given you and I are friends with Matt and Holly it seems overly formal for you to call me Ms. Galloway."

Ben smiled at Alex as he said, "Sure that seems okay as long as you call me Ben instead of Detective Canfield."

Holly and I exchanged a glance and she gave me a wink that was observed by Alex and Ben who both blushed. I covered the awkward pause with a good guffaw and said, "Got something in your eye Holly?" Holly wiped the smile off her face and said with a straight face, "My contact is bugging me jut a bit, Matt. Must be time to change them out."

We were all saved by a ringing on Ben's phone. He pulled it out of his pocket and spoke very briefly before hanging up and saying to us, "That was my guy at the station. He did not find any keys in the Peterson file. Not a surprise to any of us and I think we can all draw the same conclusions. Of course there is nothing I can take to a judge and it gets us no closer to figuring out who is behind all this." With that he stood and said, "I should probably get back to work. I need to type up a few notes related to some interviews I did earlier today."

I stood up as well and said, "I've got a venison roast and spuds in the oven and Holly is coming over to meet the two kids I've got as temporary room mates." I looked at Ben and Alex and continued by saying, "The roast is plenty big enough for six if you two want to join us. Should be ready to eat by about 6:30. Interested?"

Ben and Alex exchanged a glance and Alex said, "Sure, speaking for myself that sounds great. That would give me a little time to start picking up while I wait for the locksmith before heading over. Can I bring anything?"

Holly interjected by saying, "How about we pool our resources and throw together a big green salad, Alex?" I nodded and Alex said she thought that would be great. We all looked at Ben who said, "I should be able to wrap things up by then. How about I bring a couple of bottles of wine?"

I said, "Perfect, sounds like we're set for a feast and Joe and Christine are in for a big surprise. I'd better give them a bit of a heads up." I turned and headed to the front door and Ben and Alex followed. Alex opened the door for us and we agreed to meet again at my place at 6:30 or so. I waved to Holly before Alex closed the door.

As Ben and I walked to our cars he said, "You and Holly are quite an act, Matt. I have to admit I'm looking forward to dinner. That should be a nice way to end a trying day."

I chuckled and said, "Yeah, you'd almost think we'd rehearsed wouldn't you? Of course I just followed along and Holly is the real instigator. I'm looking forward to having you all over as well. I'll be interested to hear what you, Holly, and Alex think about Joe and Christine. I'm pretty certain they are very decent kids but sometimes I tend to kid myself and am overly optimistic."

At that point we split up and headed to separate vehicles. While I waited for him to pull out ahead of me I turned on the iPod hooked to my truck stereo and selected the Twisted Sister classic *We're Not Gonna Take it.* Seemed like the perfect song as I thought about the invasion of Alex's home and headed to my own.

XXVIII

I ARRIVED HOME AT about 5:30 and found Joe and Christine huddled around the computer. They both looked up as I walked up the stairs and Christine said, "We're looking for a twice baked potato recipe, Matt. Lot of different ones that all have a few ingredients in common. We had hoped to surprise you by having everything ready when you got home. It seems like it doesn't matter what we pick, they all sound really good. I can hardly wait until dinner."

I said, "Yeah, twice baked are some work but well worth it. I have a bit of a surprise for you. My dinner invitation got expanded to include a couple of other friends. Holly's good friend Alexandra and my friend, who happens to be a cop, Ben are also coming over. I hope you don't mind. You'll have to get used to impromptu dinner guests if you stay here very long. I like to entertain friends and do so often."

Joe and Christine both looked a bit nervous so I tried to calm their fears by continuing, "You really don't have anything to worry about. All of the people who are coming over are very good friends of mine and they are very fun people in a social setting. Don't worry for a second about Ben being a cop; he knows when not to mix business with pleasure and to be honest probably doesn't care about your past as long as you don't cross the law from here on."

That message seemed to calm both of them and Christine reached for Joe's hand and said, "Matt, you should never feel you have to explain who you have over to us but I know we both appreciate that you care enough to do so. I'm actually looking forward to meeting your friends.

If they are anything like you then it should be very fun. Now, how about you teach us how you make your potatoes?"

I thought, again, just how mature Christine was for her age and said, "Well the key to twice baked spuds is to add just enough milk but not too much. Once you get that consistency down then it comes down to putting in just the right amount of cheese, bacon and other odds and ends." With that we all trooped into the kitchen and set to work. I noticed the roast was in and the timer set. I took a quick look in the oven and was gratified by the aromatic smell of roasted meat that wafted out. When I poked the biggest potato the fork penetrated easily so I pulled all four spuds out of the oven and yelped only once as I pulled off the very hot foil. When the foil was off I cut the spuds in half long ways to get them cooling.

I pointed Joe to the cupboard where I had my small frying pan stashed and asked Christine to cut up several slices of bacon into smallish sized pieces. As they got ready I pulled the bacon and Tillamook sharp cheddar cheese out of the fridge. As Christine cut up bacon I grated cheese. Once the bacon was sizzling I directed Joe to some green onions in the fridge and asked him to chop them up. The three of us chatted cheerfully as we worked. Once things were well underway I took a moment to crank up a new music mix beginning with Rihanna which both Joe and Christine immediately recognized.

I noticed both the kids had still had lemonade going so didn't ask if they wanted anything to drink but poured myself the last of the pinot noir from the previous evening. After a sip, which was just as good as I remembered, I pulled a medium mixing bowl out of the cupboard. I tested one of the potato halves and found it was still very warm. Not having time to wait around I put on an oven mitt and set to work scoping out the insides of the spuds into the bowl. Joe and Christine watched and once I had finished I pushed the bowl over to Joe and said, "Okay, now the tricky part. Grab the milk from the fridge and pour until I say stop." He looked alarmed, undoubtedly remembering my comment from before, but did as I asked. I nodded in appreciation and hollered out "stop!" when I hoped he'd added enough.

Feeling very cheerful I pulled one of the bar stools up to the kitchen counter and said, "Okay, you guys are on your own from here on out. Just let me know if you have any questions. Everything in this kitchen is up for grabs in terms of add-ins. Don't be bashful about asking for advice."

They exchanged glances and I could see them silently agree to tackle the challenge I'd just presented them. Of course just about anything you put in twice baked potatoes comes out well, and I'd given them the basics with bacon, cheese, and green onions, but the devil is in the details. They both did very well pausing only occasionally to look at me inquiringly as they set about adding some butter, garlic, black pepper, and other odds and ends to the potato mix. Once the bacon was done they patted it free from grease and added it, the cheese and the green onions and thoroughly mixed it all up. I smiled and nodded as Christine continued without asking by pulling out a baking sheet and putting the skins on it. Joe caught on and grabbed a spoon and started piling the mixture from the bowl into the skins.

I could see the two of them were feeling pretty good as I stood up and pulled another bottle of wine, a local cabernet this time, from my wine rack. I adeptly pulled the cork, poured, and sat back down without saying a word. I couldn't help myself but began to sing along with a catchy Kelly Clarkson song. I glanced at Joe in time to see him exchange a look with Christine and heard them both break into a snicker that I took up. The three of us ended up in one of those laughing fits that left us all breathless. Joe and Christine stopped laughing abruptly and I turned to see Holly and Alex looking at us with very amused looks on their faces from the top of the stairs. Wiping a tear from my eye I managed to stop and make introductions. Once the introductions were complete the two women moved into the kitchen and said how great everything smelled. Joe, Christine and I exchanged looks but managed not to break out into laughter again.

Holly set a large wooden bowl that appeared to have an inordinate amount of good things in it on the counter and said, "Okay, here is our contribution as promised." I busied myself with getting three more wine glasses out of the cupboard. I finished off the rest of the cabernet by refilling my empty glass and filling two of the other three and gestured for us all to sit in the living room.

The five of us had barely sat down when the doorbell rang. I went down the stairs, opened the door and shook hands with Ben as he came inside. I told him, "Perfect timing, roast and spuds are just done. Come on in." He did so and followed me back up the stairs. I did the introductions as Joe and Christine stood and the three of then exchanged handshakes.

The rest of the evening went as well as it could have with good food, drink, music and camaraderie. Holly and I taught the rest of the group how to play six-handed euchre, a fast moving card game, which the four rookies enjoyed very much. The only point where the conversation turned serious is when Alex asked Holly if she could teach her how to use a hand gun. Holly, who had done a lot of shooting while growing up on her family's ranch in the Black Hills of South Dakota, readily agreed and they planned an outing for the upcoming weekend.

The group broke up at around eleven and we were all still laughing as I closed the front door behind Holly, Alex, and Ben. I went back upstairs to find Joe and Christine busily loading the dishwasher. Christine paused to say, "Matt that was so much fun. I can see why you like to have those people over. They are all very nice." Joe chimed in by saying, "That was awesome. The only downer was the women beat us at euchre but I can't wait for a rematch!"

I said, "Unfortunately in my experience the guys are more often than not on the short end of the winning side of things in cards. I keep telling myself that if I play enough over a long period of time it'll even out but sometimes I'm not so sure. Thanks for helping with the cleanup." The three of us quickly finished up and we all said goodnight.

In the roughly two minutes from my head hitting my pillow until I feel into a deep sleep I wondered what the person who had roughly searched Alex's home had been looking for. I wished that Holly was lying next to me so we could kick ideas around; she being a very practical thinker who often had good ideas. I feel asleep with her face and presence in my mind.

XXIX

My alarm went off, seeming louder than it usually did, at 6:30 the next morning. It took me a couple of minutes to remember that I had agreed to take Joe down to his new job by eight. Fortunately feeling no ill effects from the wine I'd had the night before I got up, brushed my teeth, and pulled on some sweats. I went into the kitchen and got some coffee started. I could hear the shower running so knew Joe was probably already up.

I had bagels, cream cheese, and cold cereal out by the time Joe emerged from the bathroom. We exchanged good mornings and started in on breakfast. Christine emerged from the bedroom shortly thereafter and hit the bathroom before joining us. When she was done with breakfast she got to work on making a lunch for Joe that included a sandwich of leftover venison roast and salad in a Tupperware. She asked, "Do you mind if I tag along with you and take Joe to work, Matt? I'm curious to see where the warehouse is." I told her that would be fine and the three of us headed out the door a little after 7:30.

As we drove down Vista Ave towards the river front I pointed out the nearest bus stop and the three of us agreed to pick up bus passes for the two of them later in the day. We also agreed Joe would catch the bus home after work. That settled, Christine said, "Did you hear that Holly is going to pick me up and take me shopping at around 8:30, Matt?" I responded by saying, "Nope, missed that somehow in the hubbub of the evening but that sounds good to me. Holly loves shopping and has a pretty flexible work schedule so I'm sure she is very happy to help you out."

I found it touching to see the obvious affection between the two of them as they exchanged goodbyes when we reached Joe's new work place. Once he had disappeared inside I pulled away and headed back up the hill to my house. As I drove I asked Christine, "Do you need a bit more of a loan for clothes? Don't worry about it if you do I am certain you are good for it." She smiled at me and said, "No, but thanks, I still have the forty bucks you already loaned us. Holly is taking me to Value Village and I can get a lot of good stuff very inexpensively there."

Christine and I were sharing the Portland Oregonian when Holly knocked on the door and came on up the stairs. She and I exchanged a good morning kiss and she accepted the offer of a cup of coffee. The two women exchanged shopping chit chat as we all finished off the paper and our coffee. I asked Holly if she had seen Alex and she said, "Yep, I went over early this morning and made her some breakfast. The two of us spent some time putting her house back in order. Pretty big task but Alex seemed to be in surprisingly good spirits. I think your dinner gathering did wonders for her. I also think we may have struck a good spark between Alex and Ben. Based on some of her comments I think she and Ben hit it off very well."

I grinned at her and said, "So you can add matchmaker to your resume, nice job. They seem pretty well suited to each other." Soon after that the two women headed out the door on their shopping mission and I was left alone.

I sat in the silence resulting from their departure and took up the question that had been in my mind before dropping off the night before. It seemed pretty obvious that whatever the intruder had been looking for in Alex's house had to be fairly small. I based that guess on the fact that the intruder had rifled through several small jewelry boxes on Alex's dresser and bathroom counter. I debated whether the ransacking of Alex's home could have been triggered by my visit to Ms. Peterson. I had after all been deliberately provocative in hopes of spurring some action that shed light on the case. I concluded that the timing did not add up and that the home invasion and my visit to Ms. Peterson were not directly connected.

I contemplated what to do next and ended up drawing a blank. I decided I needed to get some exercise and so headed to the club for a swim. Monique was already what I expected was her usual chipper self at the front desk. I paused to exchange some cheerful banter with her before heading to the locker room and pool. As I swam I focused my thoughts on where to go with the investigation. I decided it was worth a try to have another chat with Earl Peterson and with that decided I focused on finishing my swim with a burst. After showering, shaving, and getting dressed I decided to clean out my locker and take a load to the washer at home. I pulled into my driveway shortly thereafter and decided to check my mail in the usually disappointed hope that there would be some unexpected checks from grateful past clients. As I sorted through the typical junk mail I dropped a standard sized envelope. I leaned over to pick it up and saw that it had no return address and had been post marked the day before. My name and address were in hand written block letters.

Curious, I slit open the envelope and pulled out a bi-folded piece of paper. Tucked inside the paper was a smaller envelope with a number and the name of a large local bank typed on the outside. I felt the unmistakable outline of a key inside the smaller envelope and knew I was holding a safe deposit box key. I turned the piece of paper over and saw in the same block lettering the name Alexandra Galloway. That was it, nothing more.

My first reaction was excitement. I was pretty sure I knew who had sent the key and figured my probing had yielded this as a result. I also was pretty sure what I held in my hand was exactly what the person who had trashed Alex's home was looking for.

My second reaction was one of puzzlement. If my guess was correct and the key had been sent by Ms. Peterson why had she sent it to me and not the police? I was still pondering that while standing on the sidewalk that led from the street to my front door when Holly and Christine pulled up. Both women were chatting happily as they stepped out of Holly's blue Honda CRV and called out cheerful hellos to me. Christine said she was going inside to get cleaned up for work and she disappeared through my front door. I responded with an offhanded hello of my own and Holly immediately sensed my distraction. She headed towards me and said, "What's up, Matt?" I responded by holding out the paper with Alex's name on it. She took it and looked at me with a puzzled expression. I said, "That was in this envelope along with this," I held up the smaller envelope so that she could see the bank name and number before placing it in my pocket. She turned her gaze to me and said, "Bingo, I think what you just put in your pocket is exactly what the person who visited Alex's place was looking for. Bet a million dollars what is inside that box will go a long way towards solving the case." I smiled at her acuity and said, "No doubt and that is a very safe bet. I don't have a safe deposit box myself but I do know that most banks allow access to people on a signature list. Did Alex ever mention to you that Doug had signed her up for something like this?"

Holly shook her head no and said, "Only thing to do is give her a call. She took today off to work on putting her house back together." Holly handed back the piece of paper I'd handed her and pulled out her phone. She dialed and after a short pause said, "Hey, Alex, it's me. I'm standing in Matt's front yard. He got something very interesting in the mail today. It is a safe deposit box key and a piece of paper with your name on it. Did Doug ever ask you to sign anything bank related?" A pause and then she continued, "Well, would you be up for checking into this with Matt? I'm headed in to work and I bet he'd be over to pick you up in short order." She looked at me expectantly and I nodded in agreement. She continued, "Okay, he's on his way. Talk to you later." She closed her phone and stuck it in the back pocket of her jeans.

"You can imagine how much I want to go along with you and Alex, Matt, but I've got a meeting to talk about biking shorts design I cannot get out of." With that she leaned towards me and I put my arms around her and we exchanged a long kiss. She turned her beautiful blue eyes up to mine and said, "You be careful, okay?"

I said, "Of course I'll be careful, but how about another kiss just in case?" She laughed and gave me a playful chuck on my arm but did tilt her head up again which I took as an affirmative. We broke apart and she smiled at me and walked to her car. We exchanged waves as she drove away.

I stepped inside and heard the shower in the second bathroom running. I knocked on the door to the second bedroom anyway, received no response, entered and walked over to my desk. I pulled my keys out of my pocket and unlocked the drawer where I kept my .45 Colt which I pulled out. I checked the action to ensure the firearm was not loaded and then donned the shoulder holster and a windbreaker from the closet. I closed the drawer and headed out calling out through the bathroom door, "Hey, Christine, I'm headed out. Have a great first day at work. Just go out the backdoor when you go to work and leave it unlocked, we'll get you and Joe some keys made soon." She responded with a muffled "thanks" and I stepped outside and jumped in my truck. I paused for a moment and before heading out pulled out my phone and called Ben. He answered promptly and whistled when I told him of what I'd found in my mailbox. I asked if he was interested in meeting Alex and me at the bank and he responded by saying, "Are you kidding? That's like asking Popeye if he likes spinach. The answer is a foregone conclusion. I bet I beat you there." I chuckled and said, "Sure, that's what I figured. See you there."

It did not take long to reach Alex's house. She opened her front door before I had a chance to knock and said, "Hey, Matt, I'm ready to go." I didn't waste any time responding but turned on my heel and she followed me to the parking lot. As we walked I took the smaller envelope out of my pocket and handed it to her. She looked at it briefly before putting it in the front pocket of her jeans. We hopped in my truck and in a short time were pulling into the bank's parking lot.

I noticed Ben was as good as his word and he was waiting for us. He and I exchanged hellos and then he turned to Alex with a smile and said, "Hi, Alex, nice to see you again so soon. I hope you don't mind that Matt gave me a call?"

Alex returned the smile and said, "Of course not. This could be a big break. Might as well save some time and having a police officer present is probably good from a legal standpoint. To be honest I have never owned a safe deposit box and am not entirely sure that the bank will let me in. We'll see. Let's give it a go shall we?"

Ben and I both nodded and I motioned her to proceed. Ben and I followed her into the bank lobby where we all paused. Ben said, "Most banks have safe deposit customers go to the customer service desk and not a teller." He nodded towards a desk behind which sat a rotund man in a suit.

Alex nodded and walked over to the desk. The man stood and politely introduced himself as Paul Simmons. He asked what he could do for us. Alex introduced herself, Ben, and me without mentioning our occupations and took the envelope out of her pocket. She handed it to the man and said, "I'd like to get this safe deposit box please." The man took the envelope, looked at the number and sat down at his desk. He said, "Just a moment while I retrieve the signature card." He pulled out a large drawer and shuffled through some files before pulling out an envelope. He took out a small card, looked at it and passed a piece of paper across the desk. He said, "Please sign here." Alex did so and the man said, "Thank you Ms. Galloway. This way please."

Ben said, "Matt and I will wait for you right here, okay, Alexandra?" Alex looked over her shoulder as she walked away and arched her eyebrows as if in wonder. No doubt she was perplexed at how simple it was for her to access the safe deposit box. She and I had discussed this on the way to the bank and she had no idea how she could have been added as a signatory. We concluded Doug Peterson had somehow copied and forged her signature. As Alex disappeared to the back of the bank I followed Ben's lead and sat down in a chair set in a row with others near the bank officer's desk.

I didn't know about Ben but I was very fidgety as I waited for Alex to return. I glanced at him and he grinned at me and said, "Yep, I know what you are thinking and I'm right with you. I've got my fingers crossed that Alex doesn't come back empty handed. That would be a real let down."

We didn't have to sit and fret for very long. Alex returned from the back area of the bank after a very short wait. We both noticed that she was carrying a fairly bulky manila envelope. As they approached Alex turned and thanked the bank officer and then told him goodbye. Mr. Simmons returned the good bye and included Ben and me in a nod farewell before returning to his chair behind the desk.

As we walked across the parking lot Ben said, "Alex, I think we should be very careful in handling that envelope. I would suggest we head straight down to the precinct and formally log it as evidence in the Peterson file. I'd like to dust it and the items Matt got in the mail for prints as well."

I noticed a very brief surprised look cross Alex's beautiful face before she responded, "Of course, Ben, I should have realized this is what should be done. I was hoping we could just dig right in and solve the crime." She turned to me and said, "I assume you want to come along, Matt?" I nodded and Ben said it would be fine if I sat in.

Alex and I followed Ben out of the parking lot and down town to the Central Precinct. Ben, of course, was able to drive inside the parking garage but fortunately I had no trouble finding a spot close to the structure very near where I had parked just a few mornings ago when I had received that first call. Ben met us in the small entry area and the three of us proceeded up to the floor where we had been before. We followed Ben down a hallway and into a lab like room with a couple of men working in shirtsleeves at a long table. One of them stood up and asked Ben, "What have you got Detective?"

Ben introduced Alex and me and brought the man, whose name was Irv, up to speed on how we had obtained the contents of the safe deposit box. He concluded by saying, "So I'd like to get these items dusted for prints, Irv. Can you make it a priority? It probably is evidence in the Peterson homicide." He gestured to Alex who held out the manila envelope and smaller envelope in which she had replaced the original contents.

Irv paused to snap on some latex gloves before accepting the envelopes, which he placed in metal trays, from Alex. He asked, "Who besides you has touched these things since you got them, Ms. Galloway?"

Alex said, "No one besides me touched the manila envelope since I took it out of the safe deposit box and handed it to you. As far as the other stuff I know Matt and I both touched all of those items." I cleared my throat and interrupted, "Excuse me, Alex, but I did hand Holly the paper that has your name on it so her prints are on there as well."

Irv nodded and said, "That's not the end of the world as long as we are able to match prints with people. Mr. MacKinnon, I assume your prints are already in AFIS (automated fingerprint identification system)?" I shook my head yes. I'd been fingerprinted when I joined the Coast Guard service and applied for my concealed firearms permit application. "How about you, Ms. Galloway? Have you had occasion to be finger printed and if not would you object to doing so now?" Alex shook her head, no, and said, "I don't object at all." Irv quickly set up the live scan device and Alex's fingerprints were in the system in short order. Once that was done Irv continued, "Now, did any of you take any of the contents out of the manila envelope?" We all responded in the negative. He took some notes on a form he had on a clipboard and continued, "Okay, I'll get right on it. How about you come back in half an hour or so?"

Ben nodded and we took our leave. Ben paused in the hallway and said, "Well, we've obviously got some time to kill. I've got some paperwork to do that is associated with this business. Would the two of you mind hanging out at the Starbuck's across the street? I promise I'll give you a call the moment Irv is done with the envelope."

Alex and I agreed and Ben saw us onto the elevator which we took to the ground level. Once we exited the building we walked down half a block and crossed over to the Starbucks which had a surprisingly short line. As we approached the counter I turned to Alex and said, "Grande vanilla latte, right?" She smiled at me and said, "Your memory is good and that would be perfect. I'll get us a table." As she walked away I noticed more than a few male heads swivel to watch her progress.

I paid for the drinks and when they were done I picked them up and joined Alex. She picked up her drink and we both took appreciative sips. We were both a bit on edge but our conversation flowed very naturally and time passed quickly. I was actually a bit surprised when my phone rang and I saw it was Ben. I also noticed that nearly an hour had passed since we'd sat down. I answered and he said, "Irv is all done. Why don't you come on back and we can take a look at what we've got?" I told him we'd be right there and we stood, tossed our empties in the trash, and walked back across the street. We were met by a uniformed officer who told us Ben had asked him to meet us and escort us to the elevator. Ben was waiting for us when the elevator doors opened and he led us to the same room where his first interview of Alex had taken place.

A fit looking woman with thick gray hair and stylish gold rimmed glasses was already in the room. She stood as we entered. Ben said, "Matt and Alex, this is Sylvia Andros. Sylvia is a whiz with financial stuff and is in our fraud division. I took advantage of her being in the building to ask her to join us because Irv told me much of what was in the envelope appeared to be financial records. I told her your discretion is guaranteed." Alex and I nodded and shook Sylvia's hand before sitting down across the table from her. Ben sat down in a chair next to Sylvia.

Ben cleared his throat and said, "The run down on the prints is there are two sets, one of which Irv confirmed are Doug Peterson's, on the papers in the manila envelope. The other set is an unknown at this time. The results from the smaller envelope with the safe deposit box key are jumbled, clearly several people including Peterson and the two of you handled that item. Certainly at least one bank person but who knows. The results on the paper with your name, Alex, and the envelope you got in the mail, Matt, are more interesting. The envelope the stuff came in had three set of prints on it. Both of yours and one unidentified, presumably the sender's. The paper with Alex's name on it had four sets, yours and two others one of which matches the unidentified set on the envelope and the other probably Holly's but we don't have her prints so can't say that with certainty."

Ben turned his attention to the contents of the manila envelope which were on the table in front of him. He said, "Sylvia and I took one very brief pass through these papers while we were waiting for you to come up. As Irv thought they are copies of various financial transactions. Someone, I would venture to guess Doug Peterson, has actually taken a yellow highlighter to various transactions. Makes it pretty easy for someone unfamiliar with the contents to focus on important stuff." He turned to Sylvia and said, "Do you mind taking it from here Sylvia?"

Sylvia replied in a precise tone by saying, "Yes, Ben. Of course I haven't had time to analyze these documents completely. At first blush I see very clear documentation of skimming, significant skimming, of client accounts at Unlimited Horizons Investing. It will take me some time to determine the details and total amounts but I do see records dating back at least three years so this has been going on for some time. In my opinion, which is shared by Detective Canfield, a more detailed examination of these files will provide ample evidence that will justify a warrant to seize Unlimited Horizons records and arrest Mr. Earl Peterson and his partner."

Ben interjected to say, "Another very interesting item in the files is another name, Jonathan Clary, is highlighted several times. It appears this man was a broker for Unlimited Horizons up to about six months or so ago. At least his name doesn't show up in the records after six months ago. We'll be looking into his involvement in this affair very closely I can assure you." Ben looked directly at Alex and said, "Alex, I remember you mentioned Doug introduced you to a man named Jonathan once or twice at Portland Meadows. Does the last name Clary ring any bells? Also, would you recognize that person if you saw him again?"

Alex responded by saying, "No, I do not recognize that last name. When I was introduced that that guy at the track it was on a first name basis. I would definitely remember him if I saw him again though. He had dark hair and was maybe 5' 8" and 170 pounds give or take a bit."

There was a long pause as we all collected our thoughts and then I said, "Alex, Ben and Sylvia obviously need to jump on this so we should get out of their hair and let them do their jobs." I looked and Ben and said, "Can you give me a call when you execute the warrant? I'd like to be there to see that arrogant jerk hauled away in hand cuffs. Call me petty but that would be very satisfying."

Ben nodded and said, "Sure, I will do that. It might be tomorrow morning. There is a lot of information in these files and we of course want to make sure we have an airtight case." The four of us stood, exchanged handshakes and Ben escorted us back to the elevator. As we waited for it to arrive on our floor Alex voiced the thought that was at the forefront of my mind, "It is so sad that Doug was probably murdered because he was involved in blackmailing his father. Even if Earl didn't pull the trigger he's got to know who did and he hasn't come forward even though his own son was killed. How can people live that way?" Neither Ben nor I had any answers. None of us spoke further as the elevator arrived, Alex and I stepped inside, and we parted in silence.

XXX

THE SILENCE CONTINUED FOR most of the drive to Alex's condo. As we pulled into her parking lot I asked her if she wanted any help putting her house back together. She responded by saying, "No, but thanks, Matt. I've made quite a bit of progress already and should have it pretty well wrapped up by later today." She leaned over and we exchanged a friendly hug and she said, "Thank you so much for your support. I don't know what I'd do without friends like you and Holly."

"Sure, you are not so bad yourself and I admire you for being so level headed during this entire hullabaloo. I'm sure we'll see each other soon. Maybe at the gun range this weekend?" She nodded and said she was looking forward to that and with that hopped out of my truck and headed towards her front door.

I looked at my dashboard clock and saw it was just before three. Thinking I might be shooting with Alex and Holly, and perhaps Ben, at some point in the near future I decided to get a little practice. The range I usually shot at was up Interstate 5 just before crossing into Washington. It took me about twenty minutes to reach there after pulling out of Alex's parking area.

As I waked through the door into the facilities shop area, Mike, one of the co-owners of the range, called out a hello. I was a regular and had purchased an unlimited membership when I had moved back to Portland after getting out of the Coast Guard. Mike and I were on a first name basis and casual friends. He asked, "What are you shooting today, Matt? Sticking with your .45 or do you want to try the Sig or Glock?"

As much as I loved my .45 I had come to realize there were probably better semiautomatic pistols on the market so I had test fired a Glock-17 and a Sig Sauer P250 the last few times I'd been to the range. I'd been impressed by both firearms but could not decide which way to go.

"I'll just stick with my .45 for today, Mike. How about two boxes please?" Mike nodded and placed two 50 count boxes of .45 ammo in a plastic basket. He also put a set of headphones and eye protection in the basket, handed me three paper targets, and told me I could take lane 1.

I thanked him, put on the ear and eye protection and passed through the double set of doors and into the firing area. I spent the next hour shooting from various stances using both hands and either my left or right hands alone at different distances. When I was done all three targets had holes pretty much where I wanted the holes to be and I was content with the results. I headed back to the shop area, turned in my safety gear, paid my tab and bid good-bye to Mike.

I noticed it was a little after five so I decided to give Holly a call. She picked up her phone after a couple of rings and said, "Hi, Matt, just the person I've been hoping to talk to. What have you got going for dinner?"

It felt good to hear her voice and I responded by saying, "No plan which is exactly what I was calling about. Do you have anything in mind?"

"How about I make dinner at my house for a change?" Holly said, "I assume you feel okay leaving Joe and Christine alone at your place? If you'd rather bring them along that'd be fine too."

At that moment the thought of being alone with Holly for an evening seemed very appealing so I said, "Joe and Christine will be fine. They will have lots of catching up to do with each other with the new jobs. I've got to be comfortable leaving them on their own sooner or later and it might as well start now. What can I bring over and when should I show up?" We settled on me bringing wine and seven o'clock, Holly wanted time for a workout before we got together. That settled we exchanged fond farewells and I headed for home.

I pulled into my driveway, parked, and went in through the back door as I usually did. I knew Christine did not get off until after six and doubted Joe had time to get home via the bus yet but called out, "Anybody home?" There was no answer but I felt a hard prod in the area of my left kidney and a male voice say, "Hands behind your head right now. I am not kidding around." Whoever it was had stepped from behind the left side of the door as it opened and been waiting for me.

I clenched my teeth and cursed myself for being so stupid as to have Christine leave the door unlocked. I did as ordered and felt a hand pat down my upper body. Of course he instantly encountered the shoulder holster and he said, "Oh, boy can't have you doing anything stupid with this. Turn around, keep your hands laced behind your head and let me take a look."

I did so and turned to see a guy who was slightly shorter than me wearing a ski mask. He was holding a semiautomatic pistol in his right hand which he kept inches from my torso. He used his left hand to reach in and remove my Colt which he stuck into the front waist band of his pants underneath his belt. He said, "Good, now you turn around and go sit down in your living room. We need to have a little talk." I passed through the dining room and moved deliberately to the left towards a straight cushioned chair and away from the recliner and he said, "That's just fine. Sit. You can take you hands down once your butt hits the seat."

I turned and sat down and brought my hands to my lap. The man took a couple of steps without presenting his back to me and continued, "I think you know what I want. I'm tired of playing hid and go seek. Just give me the papers and I'm out of here."

I said, hoping to put him off balance and gain some initiative myself, "Don't you feel foolish wearing a ski mask, Jonathan? Those papers are with the cops right now and my guess is they've got a file already set up for you. You're not fooling anybody any more."

The guy cursed vehemently and tore off the mask. He yelped, "Damn it, I should have clipped that witch Anderson sooner. I knew she would spill her guts. I should have also stuck around to finish you off that night on Burnside."

I could see panic in his eyes and hoped my salvo wouldn't result in him shooting me on the spot. I continued, "You gain nothing by shooting me now and you can't possibly get out of this mess. Why don't you put down the gun and cut your losses?"

The panicked look receded. A perhaps more frightening calculating look replaced it and he said, "You must think I'm stupid. Just shut your mouth and let me think."

At that moment the back door opened and Joe came in calling out, "Hey, Matt, I'm here."

Jonathan turned half way and I took advantage of the distraction to launch myself at him grabbing for his gun hand with both of mine. A shot rang out and I felt a searing pain on my left side but I was able to get a hold of his wrist and the barrel of the gun. Jonathan, though a bit smaller than me, was strong and we struggled for control. I dimly heard Joe call out something but couldn't make it out. At that moment my world was focused solely on one thing. I felt Jonathan bring a leg up and I barely twisted aside in time to avoid a knee to my groin. I countered by letting go of Jonathan's wrist and elbowing him directly in the front of his throat. That brought him down and we both fell onto the floor. I smashed his hand down on the hardwood floor and the gun finally fell out of his grip and skittered away. At that moment Joe jumped into the fray. He quickly wrapped himself around Jonathan in a leg and head lock and the fight was over. Jonathan couldn't move.

Joe called out in a strained voice, "I've got him, Matt." I quickly grabbed my .45 from Jonathan's waistband, worked the action to chamber a round and stood up. I took a step over to the other pistol and bent down and picked it up. That accounted for I stooped and placed the barrel of my Colt hard against the back of Jonathan's skull. I said, "You are done. Let him go, Joe." Joe disengaged and I continued. "Turn face down and spread your arms and legs right now." Jonathan did so and I handed Joe the other pistol. I asked if he knew how to empty it. He did not so I talked him through it. Once the bullets were all out I had him hand them to me and I put them in my front pocket. I asked him to put the gun on the counter and continued, "There are some heavy wire ties in the lowest kitchen drawer to the right of the oven. If you'd go get them that'd be great." Joe did so and when he returned I had him zip tie Jonathan's ankles together. That done I told Jonathan to put is hands behind his back and Joe did the same with his hands.

Only then did I pull my pistol away from the back of Jonathan's head. I backed away and sat down. Joe took the chair opposite me and we looked at each other. I said, "That was impressive. Where did you learn to do that?"

Joe said, "High school wrestling. It was a great stress outlet and I was pretty good. I never won any state competitions but usually came in second or third in my weight class." His voice took on a concerned tone and he said, "Matt, you've been shot. There is blood on your left side."

I looked down and saw that there was indeed blood and a hole in my shirt. I gingerly felt the area and winced in pain but determined the bullet had just grazed my rib. No significant damage but I knew it would be painful for a while.

Jonathan chose that moment to let out a strangled snarl of fury and he thrashed and struggled against his bonds. Wire ties are very effective and he had no chance of freeing himself. I decided it was time to call in the cavalry and reached for the phone. I dialed Ben's number. He picked up and I said, "Just calling to let you know I've saved you a bit of work. Jonathan Clary is lying on my floor right now hog tied and immobile. He surprised me when I got home, we had a tussle and Joe showed up just in time to save the day. Apparently he was still looking for the papers you have. I have his gun and can't wait to see ballistics matches for the bullets from the other crime scenes."

Ben said in a startled tone, "Damn, Matt, you do have a certain flair for drama. Hold the fort, I'll be there with some help in no time." We hung up and I settled back, finally relaxing just a little bit.

I took the opportunity to ask Joe to go to the bathroom and get some gauze, tape, and other supplies. I also asked him to get me a new shirt from my bedroom. We were busy taking care of what really was a pretty minor wound when I saw two patrol cars and an unmarked sedan pull up outside, lights flashing. Soon thereafter my house was alive of police activity and I let Ben take over the show. He did so in his usual efficient manner and I knew everything would be just fine.

XXXI

It was Friday evening a week later. Holly, Alex, Ben, Joe, Christine, and I were gathered around my table eating lemon grilled fresh steelhead, home made dinner rolls, and a Caesar salad. The four of us who were old enough to imbibe had all agreed that the Pinot Gris from a Willamette Valley vineyard not too far from downtown Portland went very well with the menu. The conversation up to that point had been lighthearted and very cheerful. It became more serious when Alex asked Ben if he could provide an update on the Peterson case.

I had gotten the call from Ben the previous Friday morning before he and other officers had served the warrant on Earl Peterson at this office. I did admit that I had felt a great deal of satisfaction watching him get taken away in hand cuffs and knowing he had seen me standing outside his office. Peterson looked much less a Wall Street power broker and more a bitterly unhappy old man which almost, but not quite, left me feeling sorry for him. The timing of the arrest had been very good as Peterson had been found with a briefcase full of cash and a one way first class ticket to a place with a much warmer climate than Portland. He was busily shredding documents when the police had burst into his office quite unannounced.

Ben cleared his throat and after a sip of wine said, "Well, once he opened up it was almost hard to get Jonathan Clary to stop talking. His hatred of Earl is palpable and is rooted in his having been fired by the older Peterson. He found Doug to be a very willing conspirator in the blackmail scheme the two of them cooked up. Their endeavor might have continued for a long time but Jonathan said Doug got greedy because of horse betting debts. Jonathan told us he had to shut Doug up and killed him not only because of that but as a serious warning to the older Peterson." He paused to take another sip which I noticed left him with an empty glass. I stood, went to the fridge and opened a third bottle which I carried around the table pouring as I went. I set the bottle down on the table and sat down after making sure Joe and Christine did not need refills on their lemonade.

Ben continued, "We have an airtight case against Earl Peterson for embezzlement. The papers you recovered from the safe deposit box alone were enough, Alex, but there was a lot more evidence that Peterson hadn't had time to shred. The case of murder and two counts of attempted murder against Jonathan Clary are also airtight. We have ballistics matches from each scene with the gun Matt took away from him. The gun is actually registered in his name. Long and the short of it is those two guys are pretty cut and dried trials away from serving a long, long time behind bars.

At that I proposed a toast to a successful conclusion and we all touched our glasses together with a cheer. We put the serious topics away for the night and played euchre well into the wee hours of the morning.

It was well after ten the next mooring when I left Holly in bed, pulled on my robe, and stumbled out to the kitchen to get a pot of very strong coffee going. I walked out to get the paper and check the mail. As I thumbed through the stack I stopped in my tracks in almost exactly the same spot I'd stopped the day I'd gotten the key in the mail. I held in my hand an envelope with my name and address written in similar hand written block letters on it. The difference being there was a return address in the upper let corner. The letter had come from Mrs. Eleanor Peterson. The envelope contained a check with a very hefty sum written on it. I smiled at what seemed to be implied humor of the lettering and thought that maybe my impressions of Mrs. Peterson were not as accurate as I thought.

I went back inside and dialed her number. A very familiar voice answered the phone and I said, "Good morning, Gillian. How is your recovery going?" In a development that had surprised me I knew that Mrs. Peterson had generously told Gillian that she would cover all of her medical bills.

I could tell Gillian had a smile on her face when she responded by saying she was doing well and that her arm would probably be out of its sling after a couple of more weeks of physical therapy. I asked if Mrs. Peterson was around and soon heard her say in a tone very unlike the one I had heard her use the last time we had spoken, "Yes, Mr. MacKinnon?"

"I'm calling to inquire about the check I just received from you Mrs. Peterson. I must say it is quite unexpected."

"Mr. MacKinnon, the last time we spoke you informed me that you would be sending me a final bill. You have failed to do so up to this point so I just took a guess at what your bill might be. Is the amount not adequate?"

I smiled into the phone and said, "No, the amount is just fine and appreciated." I paused before gamely adding in an inquiring tone, "Mrs. Peterson, I haven't yet thanked you for sending me the safe deposit box key."

There was an even longer pause before she said, "Of course I don't know what you are talking about Mr. MacKinnon." Another long pause before she said, "The man was responsible for my son's death. I will live with my inactivity for the rest of my life. Good day to you Mr. MacKinnon."

As I hung up the phone I knew that chapter of my life was over. I looked at the amount of the check again and found myself wondering if Holly would be up for a king salmon fishing trip to Alaska in June. I stood up and went back to bed to ask her. She didn't fully answer the question until an hour or so later.